Sans Souci

Also by Dionne Brand

Sans Souci

and other stories

Dionne Brand

Firebrand
Books
Ithaca, New York

Several of the stories in this collection appeared previously in *Fireweed* and *Stories by Canadian Women* (Oxford University Press).

Originally published in Canada in 1988 by Williams-Wallace Publishers, Inc.

Cover art by Helena Cooper
Cover design by Mary A. Scott

Printed on acid-free paper in the United States by McNaughton & Gunn

Library of Congress Cataloging-in-Publication Data

Brand, Dionne, 1953-
    Sans souci, and other stories / by Dionne Brand.
      p.   cm.
    ISBN 0-932379-71-0 (alk. paper). — ISBN 0-932379-70-2 (pbk. : alk. paper)
      1. Women, Black—Fiction.   I. Title.
PR9199.3.B683S26   1989
813'.54—dc20   89-23614
                                                        CIP

For Faith

and to be awake is more lovely than dreams

Acknowledgments

I would like to thank Filomena Carvalho, Joyce Mason, Pat Murphy, Faith Nolan, Marlene Philip, Barb Taylor, and Roger McTair, as well as the Fireweed Collective and the Black Women's Collective for their support, advice, and comments in the development of these stories.

Dionne Brand
Toronto, 1988

Contents

Sans Souci

I

Rough grass asserted itself everywhere, keeping the earth damp and muddy. It inched its way closer and closer to doorsteps and walls until some hand, usually hers, ripped it from its tendrilled roots. But it soon grew back again. It kept the woman in protracted battle with its creeping mossiness — she ripping it out, shaking the roots of earth. It grew again the minute she turned her back. The house, like the others running up and down the hill, could barely be seen from the struggling road, covered as it was by lush immortelle trees with coarse vine spread among them so that they looked like women, with great bushy hair, embracing.

In Sans Souci, as the place was called, they said the people were as rough as the grass.

She may have looked that way, but it was from walking the hills and tearing out grass which grew until she was afraid of it covering her. It hung like tattered clothing from her hips, her breasts, her whole large body. Even when her arms were lifted, carrying water to the small shack, she felt weighed down by the bush. Great green patches of leaves, bougainvillea, almond, karili vine fastened her ankles to her wrists. She kept her eyes to the floor of the land. Her look tracing, piercing the bush and marking her steps to the water, to the tub, to the fire, to the road, to the land. The woman turning into a tree, though she was not even old yet. As time went on she felt her back harden like a crab's, like the bark of a tree, like its hard brown meat. A man would come often, but it was difficult to know him. When she saw him coming, she would never know him, until he said her name. *Claudine.* Then she would remember him, vaguely. A bee near her ear. Her hand brushing it away.

Sometimes she let the bush grow as tall as it wanted. It overwhelmed her. Reaching at her, each new spore or shoot burdened her. Then someone would pass by and not see the house and say that she was minding snakes. Then, she would cut it down.

She climbed the hill often when the bush was low around the house. Then she went for water, or so it seemed, because she carried a pot. Reaching the top, her feet caked with mud, she would sit on the ground near the edge of the cliff. Then, she would look down into the sea and rehearse her falling — a free fall, a dive into the sea. How fast the sea would come toward her. Probably not. The cliff was not vertical enough. Her body would hit tufts of grass before reaching the bottom. She could not push off far enough to fall into the water. Musing on whether it would work or not, she would lie down on the ground, confused. Spread out, the pot beneath her head, she would be faced by the sky. Then her eyes would close, tired of the blue of the sky zooming in and out at her gaze, and she would be asleep. She never woke up suddenly, always slowly, as if someone else was there, moving in on her sleep, even when it rained a strong rain which pushed her

2

into the ground or when she slept till the sky turned purple.

Her children knew where she was. They would come up the hill when they did not see her or go to their grandmother's. She never woke up suddenly here, even when the three of them screamed her name. *Claudine!* The boy, with his glum face turning cloudier, and the girl and the little boy, looking hungry. Three of them. In the beginning, she had bathed them and oiled their skins in coconut and dressed them in the wildest and brightest of colours and played with them and shown them off to the other inhabitants of the place. Then they were not good to play with any more. They cried and felt her hands. They cried for the roughness of her hands and the slap. If he was there he would either say, "Don't hit them" or "Why don't you hit those children?" His ambiguity caused her to hesitate before each decision on punishment. Then she decided not to touch the children, since either instruction he gave, he gave in an angry and distant voice, and for her the two had to be separate thoughts, clear opposites. So, after a time, the children did not get bathed and dressed and, after a time, they did not get beaten either.

The people around spoke well of him, described his physical attributes which were, in the main, two cheloidal scars on his chin and face. The scars meant that he was afraid of nothing. When he came he told them of his escapades on the bigger island. Like the time he met the famous criminal, Weapon, and he and Weapon spent the night drinking and touring the whore houses and the gambling dens and Weapon stuck a knife into the palm of a man who touched his drink.

He brought new fashions to the place, the wearing of a gold ring on his little finger and the growing of an elegant nail to set it off. The men, they retold his stories until he came with new ones. They wore copper rings on their little fingers.

If she wasn't careful, they would come into the house and tell her what to do again. The shacks up and down the hill were arranged like spiders crawling toward her. One strong rain and they'd be inside of her house — which was not at the bottom of the hill, so there was no real reason to think that it would actually happen. Looking at them, the other people, she saw they made gestures toward her as they did to each other, to everyone else. They brought her things and she gave them things and they never noticed, nor did he, that she was not her mother's child nor her sister's sister nor an inhabitant of the place, but the woman turning into a tree. They had pressed her with their eyes and their talk and their complicit winks first into a hibiscus switch, then into a shrub, and now this, a tree.

He didn't live there. The dirt path beside the house ran arbitrarily up the hill. Whenever he came, he broke a switch with which to scare the children. This was his idea of being fatherly. Coming through the path, he made his stern face up to greet the children and the woman. He came and went and the people in the place expected her to be his. They assumed this as they assumed the path up the hill, the steady rain in March. He is a man, you're a woman; that's how it is.

Those times, not like the first, he would sit on her bed like a piece of wood, his face blunt in the air, dense and unmoving. He had no memory. Almost like the first, his breathing and his sweat smelling the same hurry thickness as before. Like something which had walked for miles with rain falling and insects biting, the bush and trees slapping some green and murky scent onto its body, a scent rough, from years of instinct, and horrible. Now he grew his

4

fingernails and splashed himself with cheap scent; but sometimes, when he lifted his arm, she recalled and forgot quickly. And sometimes she saw his face as before. Always, in and out of seeing him and not seeing him, or wondering who he was and disbelieving when she knew.

Those times he would sit on her bed and tell her about a piece of land which his maternal grandmother had left him. He was just waiting for the day that they built the road across Sans Souci, and that was the day that he was going to be a rich man. It was good agricultural land, he said, and only a road was holding it back. He went on about how he would work the land and how he was really a man of the earth. She listened, even though she knew that his mouth was full of nonsense. He had said that, for the last many years.

How many? . . . was he the same as the first . . . somehow she had come to be with him. Not if he was the first, not him.

His hands with their long fingernails, the elegant long nail on the right finger, could never dig into the soil. She listened to him, even though she knew that he was lying. But he really wasn't lying to deceive her. He liked to hear himself. He liked to think that he sounded like a man of ideas, like a man going somewhere. Mostly he repeated some phrase which he heard in a popular song or something he had heard at the occasional north american evangelist meeting. He had woven these two into a thousand more convolutions than they already were, and only he could understand them — he and the other men in the place and Claudine, who couldn't really understand either, but liked the sound of him. His sound confused her; it was different, not like the pig squealing, that sorrowful squealing as it hung in front of the knife, not like its empty sound, as it hung for days, years — its white belly bloodless when

5

it hung with no one seeing it, none around except the air of the yard, folding and sealing pockets of flesh, dying. His sound covered an afternoon or so for her, above the chorus of the pig's squeal, at once mournful and brief in its urgency — the startling incident of its death mixed with commonplaceness and routine. She liked to have him sit with her as if they were husband and wife.

II

She had met Uncle Ranni on the Carenage. She never thought that he would ever get old; he used to be quick and smooth, with golden rings on his fingers. Each time he smiled or laughed — that challenging sweet laugh of his — the sun would catch the glint of his rings and throw it onto his teeth so that they looked yellow. He would throw his head way back, revealing the gold nugget on his thick chain. He was a small man, but you would never know, looking at him when he laughed.

Even when he talked of killing a man he laughed that sweet laugh, only his eyes were different. They cut across your face for the briefest of moments, like the knife that he intended to use. Once he even threatened to kill his father and his father believed him and slapped his face and never spoke to him again.

She poured everything out to him now, hoping he would kill the man this time. Everything about Prime's exhortations and his lies. It came out of her mouth, and she didn't know who was saying it. Uncle Ranni's laugh only changed slightly. No one in the family ever really believed that he'd ever kill anyone; but no one ever dared not to believe either. Something about his laugh said that he'd never kill a man if he didn't have to and if he did, it would be personal. With a knife or a machete. Never a gun, but close, so that the dying man would know who had killed him and why. She'd caught a glimpse of him once, under a tamarind tree, talking about cutting a man's head off and the eyes of the head open, as it lay apart from its body in the dirt. He had told it and the men around, kicking the dust with their toes, had laughed, weakly.

Claudine told him everything, even some things that she only thought happened. These didn't make the case against Prime any worse, they just made her story more lyrical, inspiring the challenging laugh from Ranni. "This man don't know who your uncle is, or what?" This only made her say more. Prime had lied to her and left her with three children to feed.

The new child, the fourth, moved in her like the first. It felt green and angry. Her flesh all around it, forced to hang there protecting this green and angry thing. It reached into her throat, sending up bubbles and making her dizzy all the time. It was not that she hated it; she only wanted to be without it. Out, out, out, out, never to have happened. She wanted to be before it, to never know or have known about it. He had said that the land was in her name. He had even shown her papers which said so and now he had run off, taken a boat to St. Croix.

"St. Croix? It don't have a place that man can hide; he don't know me," Uncle Ranni said. Claudine got more and more frightened and more and more excited as she talked the story. It would serve Prime right to have Uncle Ranni chop him up with a knife; she would like to see it herself. Uncle Ranni was old now. Sixty-four, but when he laughed like that she could see his mouth still full of his white teeth. It surprised her. Her mother's brother. He had looked at her once, back then, as if she had made it happen — looked at her as if she were a woman and contemptible; but it passed quickly like his other looks.

7

She'd only been talking to an old man about her trouble. She had not been paying attention. His old face had lit up briefly with that look, and his teeth were as white as when he was young. His skin was tight and black, as she remembered it years ago. He seemed to laugh out of a real joy. She remembered liking to hear him laugh and see his white teeth against his beautiful skin. He would spit afterward, as if there was something too sweet in his mouth. Now, when she'd first seen him on the Carenage, she had seen an old man with gray eyelashes and a slight stubble of gray on parts of his skin and face. She had told him everything in a surge of relief and nostalgia, never expecting him to do anything; but it was he, Uncle Ranni, she had told. She almost regretted saying anything, but she needed to say it to someone.

The look across her face as before, cutting her eyes away, cutting her lips, her head, slicing her, isolating sections of her for scrutiny and inevitable judgment. Her hand reached to touch her face, to settle, dishevelled as it was, to settle it on her empty chest. All that she had said was eaten up by the old man's face and thrown at her in a quick lacerating look which he gave back. Her eyes sniffed the quickly sealed cut and turning, fell on a wrecked boat in the Carenage.

A little boy jumped off the end not submerged in the water. The glum-faced boy at home came to her. She hurriedly made excuses to Uncle Ranni about having to go and ran with a kind of urgency toward the tied-up boat to Cast Island, disappearing into its confusion of provisions, vegetables, and goats. She did what she always had to do. She pretended to live in the present. She looked at the awful sky. She made its insistent blueness define the extent of what she could see. Before meeting Uncle Ranni she had walked along pretending that the boat was not there; that she did not have to go; wishing she could keep walking; that the Carenage would stretch out into the ocean, that the water of the ocean was a broad floor and the horizon, a shelf which divided and forgot. An end to things completely. Where she did not exist. The line of her eyes furthest look burned her face into the sunset of yellow, descending. The red appearing behind her eyelids, rubbing the line with her head. She had wished that the water between the jetty and the lapping boat was wider and fit to drink, so that she could drink deeply, become like sand, change places with the bottom of the ocean, sitting in its fat-legged deepness and its immutable width.

III

After the abortion, she went to Mama's Bar, even though she was in pain and even though she knew that she should lie down. Mama's was a wooden house turned into a restaurant and bar and Mama was a huge woman who had an excellent figure. Mama dominated the bar. She never shouted; she raised her eyebrows lazily when challenged. There were other women in the bar, regulars, who imitated Mama's walk and Mama's eyelids but deferred to Mama and faded when Mama was in the bar. Mama always sat with her back to the door, which proved just how dangerous she was.

The walls of the bar, at unaccounted intervals, had psychedelic posters in fluorescent oranges and blues. One of them was of an aztec-like mountain — dry, mud brown, cracked, strewn with human bones. Nothing stood on it except bones of feet and ribs and skulls. It would be a foreboding picture, if not for its glossiness. Instead it looked sickly and distant. It was printed by someone in

California, and one of Mama's visitors had bought it at a head shop in San Diego. Mama thought that it was high art and placed it so that people entering the bar could see it immediately.

Claudine walked down the steps to the bar, closed her eyes, anticipating the poster, then opened them too soon and felt her stomach reach for her throat.

Mama's eyes watched her walk to the counter, ask for a rum, down it and, turning to leave, bump into the man with the limp. A foamy bit of saliva hung onto the stubble on his face. He grabbed Claudine to save himself from falling and then they began dancing to Mama's crackling stereo.

They danced until lunch time, until the saliva from the limping man's face stretched onto the shoulder of Claudine's dress. Mama had not moved either. She controlled all of it with her eyes, and when they told Claudine to leave, she sat the man with the limp onto a stool and left. Going somewhere, averting her stare from the mountain strewn with human bones.

IV

She went to the address on the piece of paper someone had given her. 29 Ponces Road. When she got to the street there was no number on any of the houses. She didn't know the woman's name. It was best in these situations not to know anyone's name or to ask anyone where. She walked up and down the street looking at the houses. Some were back from the curb and faced the next street over so there was no way of telling. Maybe something about the house would tell her. What does a house where a woman does that look like, she asked herself.

She walked up and down the street thinking that maybe it was this one with the blue veranda or that one with the dog tied to a post. No, she couldn't tell. Maybe this was a sign or something. She gave up, suddenly frightened that it may just be a sign — holy mary mother of god — and bent her head, walking very fast up the street for the last time. She passed a house with nine or ten children in the yard. Most of them were chasing after a half-dressed little boy. They were screaming and pointing at something he was chewing. She hadn't seen the woman on the wooden veranda until one of the children ran toward her saying something breathless and pointing to the woman. Then she saw her, as the woman on the veranda reached out into the yard and hit a flying child. It didn't seem as if she wanted to hit this one in particular or any one in particular. The group of children gave a common flinch, accustomed to these random attacks on their chasing and rushing around, then continued after the boy. Faced with finally doing this, Claudine didn't know anymore. She hesitated, looked at the woman's face for some assurance. But nothing. The woman looked unconcerned, waiting for her, and then turned and walked into the ramshackle house, her back expecting Claudine to follow. Claudine walked toward the yard not wanting to stand in the street. Now she moved forward because of the smallest reasons; now she was trapped by even tinier steps, by tinier reasons. She moved so that her feet would follow each other, so that she could get away from the road, so that she could make the distance to the house, so that it would be over. Nothing had come from the woman's face, no sign of any opinion. Claudine had seen her face, less familiar than a stranger's. Later, when she tried, she would never remember the face, only a disquieting and unresolved meeting.

11

Like waking in between sleep and catching a figure, a movement, in the room.

V

He had raped her. That is how her first child was born. He had grabbed her and forced her into his little room and covered her mouth so that his mother would not hear her screaming. She had bitten the flesh on his hand until there was blood and still he had exploded her insides, broken her. His face was dense against her crying. He did it as if she was not there, not herself, not how she knew herself. Anyone would have seen that he was killing her, but his dense face told her that he saw nothing. She was thirteen. She felt like the hogs that were strung on the limbs of trees and slit from the genitals to the throat. That is how her first child was born.

With blood streaming down her legs and feeling broken and his standing up and saying, "Nothing is wrong, go home and don't tell anyone." And when she ran through the bush crying that she would tell her mother and stood at the stand pipe to wash the blood off her dress and to cool the pain between her thighs, she knew she could tell no one.

Up the hill to the top, overlooking the water, she wanted to dive into the sea. The water would hit her face, it would rush past her ears quickly; it would wash her limbs and everything would be as before and this would not have happened — a free fall, a dive, into the sea. No. Her body would hit tufts of grass before reaching the bottom and it would hurt even more. She could not push off far enough to fall into the water.

She said nothing. She became sick and puffy and her

stepfather told her mother that she was pregnant and she begged her mother not to believe him, it was a lie, and her mother sent her to the doctor and told her not to come back home if it was true. When the doctor explained the rape, he said, "Someone put a baby in your belly." And she could not go home. And when it was dark that night and she was alone on the road because everyone — her aunt first and then her grandmother — had said, "Go home," she saw her mother on the road coming down with a torchlight. Her mother, rakish and holding her skirt, coming toward her. Both of them alone on the road. And she walked behind her all the way home silent, as her mother cursed and told her that she'd still have to do all the work and maybe more. Every day until the birth, her mother swore and took care of her.

He denied it when the child was coming and she screamed it was "you, you, you!," loud and tearing, so that the whole village could hear that it was he. He kept quiet after that, and his mother bore his shame by feeding her and asking her, "How things dou dou?"

From then, everyone explained the rape by saying that she was his woman. They did not even say it. They did not have to. Only they made her feel as if she was carrying his body around. In their looking at her and their smiles which moved to one side of the cheek and with their eyelids, uncommonly demure or round and wide and gazing. She came into the gaze of all of them, no longer a child — much less a child who had been raped. Now, a man's body. All she remembered was his face, as if he saw nothing when he saw her, and his unusual body resembling the man who slaughtered pigs for the village — so gnarled and horrible, the way he moved. Closing her eyes, he seemed like a tamarind tree, sour and unclimbable. Her arms could not move, pinned by his knotted hands and she could not breathe. Her breathing took up all the time and she wanted to scream, not breathe — more screaming than breathing.

That is how her first child with him was born. Much as she tried, her screaming did not get past the bush and the trees; even though she tried to force it through the blades of grass and the coarse vines. Upon every movement of the bush, her thin and piercing voice grabbed for the light between. But the grass would move the other way, making the notes which got through dissonant and unconnected, not like the sound of a killing.

Train to Montreal

She sat as close as she could to the piano. The room, packed, indicated with its silence the pianist's hands anticipating the keys. Taylor had misplaced his shoes, refused to begin until he had found them. Finally, he came out, looking very annoyed. The crowd had not dared to act displeased at the delay. Now, he sat at the piano and began playing.

At first she could not figure it out. It was a theorem of some kind, more and more difficult as he rose and walked to the open belly of the piano, plucking the strings in the same clusters as with his fingers depressing the keys. The clusters sounded angry, more than angry, disturbed. Lone notes, deterring them in the middle, tolerant; patience darkened by the clustered ruptures. She felt herself plunge into the theorem, its shape, tight at first, but upon gaining entry, bounding out to full breath — the point beyond which dancers could leap — each note full breath. Here, she rode, swam a liquid distance. Air dripping from her shoulders, she heard the sound of her voice saying something, joining the note.

"What?" The man beside her. She did not hear him. The clusters came again, tight and rolling, half-gesturing, squeezing her; she, leaping to escape the end of them. "What did you say?" The man nudging her, bringing his lips close to her ear, brought her out of the music. She remembered his lips from earlier that evening and turned to him suddenly feeling drunk and tired. She looked around to see if anyone else had heard the music. It was impossible to tell. But there it was, all laid out in this blueprint which she heard. She would understand it for all the time that she could think of. The smoke and the beer blurred her vision. She leaned over to kiss the man beside her. He seemed startled, embarrassed at her gesture. "I don't understand that." She did not ask him if it was the music or the proffered kiss. One and the same. A sadness enveloped her. It was the sadness of knowing this thing which she learnt a moment ago. It was all laid out. To plunge into the theorem was to go mad. If she never got out, it was to go mad; but if she did, what was real and small and grasping, awaited. Time passed. The man said, "Are you staying for the second set? Frankly I can't get into it."

"The problem with you is that everything passed you by. I heard Malcolm. Angela went to jail. Now, all of it is in this little room and that is what you're listening to and you don't understand."

She fell back into her chair, paying no attention to his offended face, feeling half-sorry for saying it. Earlier that evening she had felt there was something important between them. Perhaps she had ruined it now. He tried to say something; the applause interrupted him. She was sure that he did not know what had offended him. "Ah, he should be more offended by what he does not understand than by me." Looking at him, unable to make up his mind whether to stay or go, she decided not to reassure him. She turned to the woman next to her to speak. Out of the corner of her eye she saw him still sitting there. She ordered another beer just to make it clear to him that she was staying. It was the intermission. Everyone was slapping their legs, the smell of perfume and beer made her a little nauseous. The man across from her was waiting for some kind of apology. She refused to give it. Jazz concerts always threw her into a pit of a mood. After, she would come out, a wry smile jerking the muscles on her face, as if some accustomed tragedy had occurred. It had been replayed; an escape had been rehearsed and outside nothing had changed. She would emerge looking at the city, shouting, sometimes aloud. Thinking of this, her mood lightened. She offered her beer to the uncomfortable man beside her. He took it reluctantly, not wanting to inspire another outburst, understanding it to be a peace offering. "You're not an asshole, not a complete asshole," she thought.

Taylor had found his shoes and began playing a piece, the islamic morning prayer. The man beside her leaned in saying something about a ride to Downsview and standing up to go. She waved to him as he squeezed past the table. Underneath the careless wave she was put out at his insensitivity to the music, never mind his insensitivity to her. Emptying the beer at her lips, feeling the last warm froths, she thought of him. She had expected him to go home with her again. She attended closely to the music.

She stood in the ticket line at Union station. The train would leave at 5:15; she would get to Montreal at 10:00 p.m. Union station, a cavern of dull heels on concrete, stunning flourescent lights, and chrome sticks, marking where to stand.

She had a new plan. Jay had called her out of the blue and

17

here she was, going to Montreal. When he moved to Montreal, fresh possibilities seemed to emerge. She needed a breather from juggling the two men in Toronto. She had told one that she would be with her sister in Scarborough and that she would not be able to see him on the weekend. What was the sense in hurting his feelings? One thing had nothing to do with the other, really. She had not seen the other since the music. She never told either of them about the other. She could handle it better than they could. This reasoning came to her again as she stood in the line to purchase her ticket. It seemed logical to her. If they found out about each other, there would be one of two consequences. They would either leave her or each would begin to press her to leave the other. Neither of these seemed sensible or possible without some discomfort.

The ticket line moved quickly. Jay would be waiting at the other end for her. At least he liked jazz. Regardless of what had happened between them before, he was pretty, with his tall slender body. Sometimes she could not believe that he was her lover. She was not particularly attractive, small and skinny, which made for her disbelief; but, he seemed not to notice and when they made love the outlines of her body seemed larger, more voluptuous than her spare frame. The occasions of their lovemaking occupied her now as she absently gave her money, took her ticket, noticed a white man in a red or black coat, gold buttons perhaps, directing her to the stairs. Lying with Jay, she imagined herself a large fruit, full, bursting at its shoulders. She looked forward to him sinking his mouth into her, like a fruit eaten.

How full the train was. It was not until the third or fourth carriage that she found an empty seat. She was surprised, really shocked at all the white faces on the train. Ridiculous of course. It was amazing, given all this time, how alarmed she still was at the sight of white faces. In the city, she hardly looked. She moved quickly along noticing only what was there, only what concerned her. Oh God, she thought, she had not noticed a single Black face to sit with. She anticipated all the other seats, except the one beside her, filling up; the furtive eyes at her, their longing for her removal, then someone without a choice sitting next to her. "Christ!"

She was looking forward to Montreal, to seeing Jay. She swallowed him. A long drink of water, her nostrils recalling his smell, secret and liquid. She felt gluttonous thinking of his body. Perhaps there would be a better place to ask him if he would live with her. A change of venue. Once, she had asked him and he had said no; and once, when she took him to see the pianist, as she took them all, she had overheard him making a date with the singer. He had not even listened, and there he was making arrangements with the singer. She'd felt ill. She had invited him to see the other side of her, to bring them closer. He had come and left with someone else. She never thought that people were that cunning. She was always startled by the things they thought of at the most odd moments. It would take her months sometimes to get to the point, to think of responses where other people knew right away what was happening and what to say. That it would strike him to make a date with the singer while the music was playing seemed to her incredibly out of place; how he noticed anyone except the music was beyond her.

Later they had a fight and he acted as if he was in control. She was in fact three years older than he and before this he had listened attentively to everything that she said. After the fight, there was the business of coming to get his records and his clothes. This was the ritual after all of her lovers. The phone call after the fight, the voices feigning emotionlessness, the conversation around the logistics of picking up the books and the records, the chance to see each other for supposedly the last time and then to forget the fight or decide that you had had quite enough of each other. This had been a pattern of hers, except for one, when she was younger, whom she stayed away from for two years after and burnt his clothing — even the T-shirt with the elephant, which she had kept longest. She imagined, though it never was true of him, that the elephant was his hope for inner gentleness.

The train pulled out and someone finally sat beside her. The carriage was not as she had imagined it. She thought that it might be like the inside of a plane, but it seemed closer. The walls were not so heavily insulated and the noise of the wheels on the track was gritting and steely.

The latecomer, male, had a guitar and reddish hair. He was short and hippie-like. She relaxed; she'd met his type. He reminded her of many years ago, "White liberals. . . when the shit starts to fly, they'll leave you in the street." She took this note of him with derision and ease.

He said that he was going to Kingston, that he used to write and sing and that he was now working as merchant marine like his father. He was writing a book. She was glad that he had sat beside her. They talked about the old days, the Soviet Union and the United States. He said that the superpowers were going to blast us all to hell. Maoist, she thought. She said that the Soviet Union never did anything to Black people. He said that he was a bit of a pacifist now. They talked until Kingston, a jarring kind of talk.

"And besides, who supported us in Africa? The United States never gave us any weapons. It's them that we're fighting."

And he, "I abhor violence of any kind. I don't care which side you're on."

"God!"

"I just don't know about that sort of action," not noticing her response.

She exhaled wearily. Jesus, why was she talking to him about Africa!

"In Germany, where was the history for it?" He looked to the ceiling of the train earnestly, then at her.

"I don't know, I wasn't there. Germany, now or then, is not a place that I understand," she replied, looking at him as if to ask, Do you?

"Well, what did it accomplish?" he, continuing, "It seems useless and wasteful to me, at any rate — kidnappings, bombings."

She was regretting talking to him. He was so comfortable with himself. And after all, she thought, what had he done — probably worn flowers in his hair and played his guitar. That was easy enough. He probably loved his father; this odd musing crossed her mind. She hated him already. She realized that she had hated him, even before he came onto the train. At the corner of her eye, she noticed his face, like a child's with its conceit, its petulance. She envied him, suddenly. She heard words coming out of her mouth despite herself.

"That may be wasteful, as you say, but you don't know what makes people do things, finally. I guess anything is useless in the face of brute strength. So I suppose we can't do anything right?"

She turned to the passing darkness outside the train, wishing that she had never talked to him. The snow, icy through the gray air, made her feel tenuous for a moment. This was to be the colour of the rest of the year's days. The train approached another tunnel, the window went black to her eyes.

"I still say they turned people off instead of. . .look, so

21

they kidnapped the guy and the multinationals get some good publicity!''

She turned to his face which had become warmer. He was so sure. Of what? she wondered. He had a calmness in his body, as if he counted on being in the world forever. He was right, she supposed. Looking at him made her feel temporary, volatile. These people, she thought, they have more patience than I. She was always afraid of bursting, a thin flame, burnt out, quickly. In his look of firmness and belonging, she understood that she owned nothing. There would always be a sadness with her; a desire to have it destroyed. It seemed hundreds of years long. It was a plump, well-fed torturer. It smacked its lips, drinking her like water, distilling her. His face was clean of any such memory. He waited for her response.

"I suppose that you can say that. I only regret that they got caught. What base are you talking about anyway? People know more about televisions and jeans than they do about what's happening right around the corner. So, if anybody acts as if they *don't* live alone in the world. . . if anybody acts as if they care about anything else, there's something wrong with them."

They both fell silent, watching the darkness outside the train again. Her long speech had trailed off looking at his face. It had exhausted her and she wasn't sure if it had made any sense or whether she wanted it to be understood.

"I know someone who was asked to join a cell here. She said that she didn't because they didn't know what they were doing."

"But that's my point exactly."

She continued, ignoring him, "Because it's easier for you people. With us, they don't have to justify anything to blast us away. Look at the Panthers. Where would I be if they hadn't done anything?"

It was freezing in the train. The smell of stale cigarettes and damp clothing enveloped the carriage. The wheels of the train ground on the brittle rails. Silence again. They were both uneasy with each other. He, convinced that she was wrong; she, finding him so settled in the comfort of his skin — his camouflage here, in the train, and in the city. It saved him the effort of decisions. He hid in it. She wanted to agree with him, but she could not. It would not be the same thing that they were agreeing to.

They spoke less and less as the three hours to Kingston passed. She reprimanded herself for talking to him. She felt that she had been duped into revealing her opinions. It would have been best to keep quiet instead of giving this white boy so much effort.

The train pulled into Kingston. He untangled himself from his half-lotus and gathered his bags up busily. She looked at him; he seemed to have shaken off their conversation already. Relieved, slinging his bag over his shoulders, he hurried up the thin path between the seats. She watched him go, a little anxiously. How like these people to suddenly turn and be strangers, as if conversation only filled up time through something which they were sure belonged to them and was unchangeable. They could return to it; she looked to nothing, an emptiness to be made or to fall into. She watched him go.

She tried to settle herself into her seat with the same uneasy feeling that she had when she boarded the train in Toronto. She closed her eyes, trying to sleep, wishing that she had gone to the washroom while the Irish hippie was still there. She would have felt safer going and coming back to her seat. Right now, she did not know if she could find her way back. She had not looked at anyone else in the carriage. His was the only face that she had memorized. The pressure in her lower abdomen became uncomfortable as she now sat, noticing the hum at first and then, the loudness of the conversations around her. The light above her head shone badly on her. She noticed that only now that he was gone. She had just opened her eyes for the first time on the train. Their corners felt tight, as if she had to rub sleep out of them.

They were pee-wee hockey teams with their parents and teachers going to Montreal. The children, no more than twelve years old. Bags and sticks lay in the aisleway. She was always afraid of white children, meeting them on the street corners. She asked herself, how can you be afraid of children? Where she grew up it was a sign of insolence to look adults in the eye. These children stared blankly and rudely at her. They were singing.

At first their voices sounded like children's, but then she heard a raucousness, a kind of sneer in the way they sang. Then she understood and was frightened. They were singing, "Wops and frogs, Montreal is full of frogs." She understood and was less willing to get up from the gray vinyl seat. The wheels of the train cackled to the song of the children. She wanted to stand, go to the washroom; but the song frightened her, made her sit still. Maybe they would see her and start singing; maybe they didn't see her yet. She should stand up before they did, before they started singing about "Wops and niggers." She had crossed her legs, until their inner softness was bruised from folding and unfolding. She had to stand, walk to the washroom. Standing was unsteady. She had sat for three hours on the train and had not felt the rocking. Her legs felt like a swimmer's, coming out of the salty water after a long time, heavy and exhausted, tied to the gravity of the sea.

She walked, not looking but feeling the eyes of strangers turning toward her. She disturbed the little vignettes of white people sleeping or reading in their seats. Faces turned quickly toward her and away. Was there annoyance in their looks? This was a bad decision. Suppose she couldn't find the washroom? Suppose she could not find her way back? Past one cabin, past another from which smoke, beer, white men's voices blasted out. From this one she caught a grimy tableau, a smell of sweat. Eyes lighting up into a leer at her passing. Quickly.

Fear, spreading fern-like through her. Maybe they would grab her, kill her, who knows. The washroom. Now, quickly, quickly. With the loud chortling of the train in her ear, then through the gauntlet of children, hockey sticks, and eyes. Back in her seat, she raised her hand to her hot face. She tried to make her breathing even, closing her eyes, separating herself from the train. Opening them, finding the dark window passing, she stared out at the crawling winter. She tried to think of Jay again, but she could not conjure his body, her sense of him; both slipped her. Using her tongue, her temples, for some memory of him. None stayed. Cold hung around him; his unimagined body, dry, unattached.

She had fallen into a nervous sleep, with the noise of the train. The children's voices woke her. It was Montreal. She had dreamt something which she could not remember. In her half-sleep, going to the dream and coming back to the dull interior of the train, something about a stone and the sea. Something about a stone and the sea, clusters, notes of water, dry rock, water, dry rock. . . . The train lit up. There were shouts and movement, baggage being pulled. The hockey cheer which had awakened her rose from the children, again. The dark window scraped the chalky insides of the train station.

As it came to a stop, she waited for the aisles to fill up and pass her. Taking her bag, she stood, disoriented as the door opened and the platform received the other passengers. Finally, she too spilled out of the door into the hurting light

25

of the low-ceilinged station. She tried to recover her former enthusiasm for the trip. Jay would be glad to see her. There was the entire weekend to make love to him and convince him. Of what, she would remember when she saw him. Then the music . . . jazz. She was not going to press him too closely. A little of the excitment returned though with the taste in her mouth. She wondered what the dream meant, about the stone.

She hurried toward the noise of the escalator following the passengers. Watching a group of white men ahead of her, her steps slowed, became wary, recognizing the group in the bar cabin. All of them, gray-suited, heavyset, huge. Business men. She hesitated, almost stopping, disturbing the flow of passengers heading for the escalator.

The group was moving slowly, laughing, slapping each other on the back, gray-suited and red-faced. Their drunkenness alarmed her. She looked down. Her eyes caught the sight of their shoes, sturdy, black or brown, expensive. The thing would be to walk past quickly or to lag behind waiting for the men to go. White men, something told her, were even more dangerous when they were drunk. She recognized in their raucousness, something of the children, something violent, something which her senses had become attuned to over the years. She must decide. Walk past or wait. Then, too late to hide among the other people, she decided — walking quickly. She looked around. There was no other exit. Quickly, she joined a new wave of passengers thinner than the first. As they approached the group of white men, the wave divided leaving her with three or four people near the platform's edge. "Hello, Darlin." A gray suit, a white beefy shirt, an arm reaching out. Coming close to her, almost touching her face — the fat hand, hair on the back like a fat worm, dangling in her face. She quickened her pace instinctively.

It didn't have to be her, that he meant. There were other people there. She estimated the width of the platform and found herself close to the train again. There was laughter from the other men. Fright running through her chest and arms. She saw a face, close to her, but far, huge, white, red, rolling on a thick neck and a mouth, open and sour. She thought of running, but her legs felt spidery. To the escalator. She would be safe among the other passengers. Finally, she met the escalator, then "Nigger whore!" a rough voice behind yelled hoarsely. She kept walking, slightly stumbling onto the clicking stairs. "Whore! Nigger! Whore!" His voice sounded as if he was cleaning phlegm from the bottom of his throat. "Nigger whore!" She placed herself among the others, climbing the escalator. They were silent. She, trying to hide, to be invisible, turning her head to see where he was, wondering how to move herself, her head, without being noticed. Her ears ringing as if slapped, she saw the crowd, some smiling at the obscene cough, others looking straight ahead. She turned away. Inside her, "Why me. Why me. Please let the escalator end. Please!" Then as she neared the top, she looked back at the endless stair. The man's voice still coughed, "Whore! Nigger-whore!"

She looked back to say something, but only said it in looking. Apologising to her past for not striking him or cursing back, for not hurting, wounding all of them standing on the escalator.

Reaching the top, she looked for her lover. She would tell Jay. No. She could not. He would get into some kind of trouble. Unable to shed the revulsion she had just felt, she attempted a smile. Jay, standing not far from the escalator, leaned against a column, newspaper in hand. She looked at his cap, at the paper in his hand, and not at his eyes. He smiled in greeting. Nothing had just happened to him as it had to her. He smiled in greeting. Nothing had just happened to him as it had to her. He smiled, happy to see her and ready to hear her news. "How are you? What's happening?" She turned back again. They had all melted into the general crowd at the station. She scanned the crowd, wondering if they remembered now, greeting their friends. They looked safe, as clothed in their friendships as the man who got off at Kingston. He had forgotten their conversation and gone back to his life. They had forgotten her humiliation.

"How are you? It's so good to see you." Jay, grabbing her shoulders.

She did not speak. She tried to smile, raising her eyebrows and cheeks with discomfort.

"I've got a car, how was the train?"

"Okay. But maybe I'll go back on Monday by plane, instead. I can't stay as long as I thought."

I should have yelled and screamed. I should have answered, cursed, smashed his mouth. I should have killed him. This, bursting against her head and hot face. She followed. Unconsciously. Letting Jay take her bag and her shoulders. She tried to get the feeling back into her legs, by walking firmly. She had let herself be humiliated without saying a word. She had been astonished, not known what to say. Astonishment. The moment on the escalator. The silence of the others. The voice spitting up. The smiles. Just that moment when she looked back, hearing the rough, click, grind, hardness of the sound under her feet, sinistering to her ears like a shell pink, fleshy, red leering. The man's face.

Her arms, fingers, body felt far away from her, as a thing which she saw but did not. Sharp, glassy coldness in her throat as she turned to her lover, taking his mouth, to break the hardness of her lips. Kissing him to recover herself. She

28

saw herself looking from a distance. The iciness of it still reached to her legs. Only anger was close, at her mouth.

Blossom, Priestess of Oya, Goddess of Winds, Storms, and Waterfalls

Blossom's was jumping tonight. Oya and Shango and God and spirit and ordinary people was chanting and singing and jumping the place down. Blossom's was a obeah house and speakeasy on Vaughan Road. People didn't come for the cheap liquor Blossom sell, though as night wear on, on any given night, Blossom, in she waters, would tilt the bottle a little in your favour. No, it wasn't the cheap liquor, even if you could drink it all night long till morning. It was the feel of the place. The cheap light revolving over the bar, the red shag covering the wall against which Blossom always sit, a line of beer along the windowsill behind, as long as she ample arms spread out over the back of a wooden bench. And the candles glowing bright on the shrine of Oya, Blossom's mother Goddess.

This was Blossom's most successful endeavour since coming to Canada. Every once in a while, under she breath, she curse the day she come to Toronto from Oropuche, Trinidad. But nothing, not even snarky white people, could keep Blossom under. When she first come it

was to babysit some snot-nosed children on Oriole Park-
way. She did meet a man, in a club on Henry Street in Port-
of-Spain, who promise she to take care of she, if she ever
was in Toronto. When Blossom reach, the man disappear,
and through the one other person she know in Toronto she
get the work on Oriole.

Well Blossom decide long that she did never mean for
this kinda work, steady cleaning up after white people,
and that is when she decide to take a course in secretarial at
night. Is there she meet Peg and Betty, who she did know
from home, and Fancy Girl. And for two good years they
all try to type; but their heart wasn't in it. So they switch to
carpentry and upholstering. Fancy Girl swear that they
could make a good business because she father was a joiner
and white people was paying a lot of money for old-
looking furniture. They all went along with this until Peg
say she need to make some fast money because where
they was going to find white people who like old furniture, and who was going to buy old furniture from Black
women anyway. That is when Fancy Girl come up with the
pyramid scheme.

They was to put everybody name on a piece of paper,
everybody was to find five people to put on the list and
that five would find five and so on. Everybody on the list
would send the first person one hundred dollars. In the
end everybody was to get thousands of dollars in the mail
and only invest one hundred, unless the pyramid break.
Fancy Girl name was first and so the pyramid start. Lo and
behold, Fancy Girl leave town saying she going to Montreal
for a weekend and it was the last they ever see she. The
pyramid bust up and they discover that Fancy Girl pick up
ten thousand dollars clean. Blossom had to hide for months
from people on the pyramid, and she swear to Peg that if
she every see Fancy Girl Munroe again, dog eat she supper.

Well now is five years since Blossom in Canada and nothing ain't breaking. She leave the people on Oriole for some others on Balmoral. The white man boss-man was a doctor. Since the day she reach, he eyeing she, eyeing she. Blossom just mark this down in she head and making sure she ain't in no room alone with he. Now one day, it so happen that she in the basement doing the washing and who come down there but he, playing like if he looking for something. She watching him from the corner of she eye and, sure as the day, he make a grab for she. Blossom know a few things, so she grab on to he little finger and start to squeeze it back till he face change all colour from white to black and he had to scream out. Blossom sheself start to scream like all hell, until the wife and children run downstairs too.

It ain't have cuss, Blossom ain't cuss that day. The wife face red and shame and then she start to watch Blossom cut eye. Well look at my cross nah Lord, Blossom think, here this dog trying to abuse me and she watching *me* cut eye! Me! a church-going woman! A craziness fly up in Blossom head and she start to go mad on them in the house. She flinging things left right and centre and cussing big word. Blossom fly right off the handle, until they send for the police for Blossom. She didn't care. They couldn't make she hush. It don't have no dignity in white man feeling you up! So she cuss out the police too, when they come, and tell them to serve and protect she, like they supposed to do and lock up the so-and-so. The doctor keep saying to the police, "Oh, this is so embarrassing. She's crazy, she's crazy." And Blossom tell him, "You ain't see crazy yet." She run and dash all the people clothes in the swimming pool and shouting, "Make me a weapon in thine hand, oh Lord!" Blossom grab on to the doctor neck, dragging him, to drown him. It take two police to unlatch

Blossom from the man red neck, yes. And how the police get Blossom to leave is a wonder. But she wouldn't leave without she pay, and in cash money too besides, she tell them. Anyhow, the police get Blossom to leave the house; and they must be 'fraid Blossom too, so they let she off down the street and tell she to go home.

The next day Blossom show up on Balmoral with a placard saying the Dr. So-and-So was a white rapist; and Peg and Betty bring a Black Power flag, and the three of them parade in front of that man house whole day. Well is now this doctor know that he mess with the wrong woman, because when he reach home that evening, Blossom and Peg and Betty bang on he car, singing, "We Shall Not Be Moved" and chanting, "Doctor So-and-So is a Rapist." They reach into the car and, well, rough up the doctor — grabbing he tie and threatening to cut off he balls. Not a soul ain't come outside, but you never see so much drapes and curtain moving and swaying up and down Balmoral. Police come again, but they tell Doctor So-and-So that the sidewalk is public property and as long as Blossom and them keep moving they wasn't committing no crime. Well, when they hear that, Blossom and them start to laugh and clap and sing "We Shall Overcome." That night, at Peg house, they laugh and they eat and they drink and dance and laugh more, remembering the doctor face when they was banging on he car. The next day Blossom hear from the Guyanese girl working next door that the whole family on Balmoral, Doctor, wife, children, cat, and dog, gone to Florida.

After that, Blossom decide to do day work here and day work there, so that no white man would be over she, and she was figuring on a way to save some money to do she own business.

Blossom start up with Victor one night in a dance. It

ain't have no reason that she could say why she hook up with him except that in a dance one night, before Fancy Girl take off, when Peg and Betty and Fancy Girl was in they dance days, she suddenly look around and all three was jack up in a corner with some man. They was grinding down the Trinidad Club and there was Blossom, alone at the table, playing she was groovin' to the music.

Alone. Well, keeping up sheself, working, working and keeping the spirits up in this cold place all the time. . . . Is not until all of a sudden one moment, you does see youself. Something tell she to stop and witness the scene. And then Blossom decide to get a man. All she girl pals had one, and Blossom decide to get one too. It sadden she a little to see she riding partners all off to the side so. After all, every weekend they used to fête and insult man when they come to ask them to dance. They would fête all night in the middle of the floor and get tight on Southern Comfort. Then they would hobble down the steps out of the club on Church or Room at the Top, high heels squeezing and waist in pain, and hail a taxi home to one house or the other. By the time the taxi reach wherever they was going, shoes would be in hand and stockings off and a lot of groaning and description of foot pain would hit the door. And comparing notes on which man look so good and which man had a hard on, they would cook, bake, and salt fish in the morning and laugh about the night before. If is one thing with Blossom, Peg and Betty and Fancy Girl, they like to have a good time. The world didn't mean for sorrow, and suffering don't suit nobody face, Blossom say.

So when she see girl-days done and everybody else straighten up and get man, Blossom decide to get a man too. The first, first man that pass Blossom eyes after deciding was Victor and Blossom decide on him. It wasn't the first man Blossom had, but it was the first one she decide to keep. It ain't have no special reason either; is just when Victor appear, Blossom get a idea to fall in love. Well, then start a long line of misery the likes of which Blossom never see before and never intend to see again. The only reason that the misery last so long is because Blossom was a stubborn woman and when she decide something, she decide. It wasn't even that Blossom really like Victor because whenever she sit down to count he attributes, the man was really lacking in kindness and had a streak of meanness when it come to woman. But she figure like and love not the same thing. So Blossom married to Victor that same summer, in the Pentecostal Church. Victor wanted to live together, but Blossom say she wouldn't be able to go to church no more if she living in sin and if Victor want any honey from she, it have to be with God blessing.

The wedding night, Victor disappear. He show up in a dance, in he white wedding suit, and Blossom ain't see him till Monday morning. So Blossom take a sign from this and start to watch Victor because she wasn't a hasty woman by nature. He come when he want, he go when he want, and vex when she ain't there. He don't bring much money. Blossom still working day work and every night of the week Victor have friends over drinking Blossom liquor. But Blossom love Victor, so she put up with this type of behaviour for a good few years; because love supposed to be hard and if it ain't hard, it ain't sweet, they say. You have to bear with man, she mother used to say, and besides, Blossom couldn't grudge Victor he good time. Living wasn't just for slaving and it seem that in this society the harder you work, the less you have. Judge not lest ye be judged; this sermon Blossom would give to Peg and Betty anytime they contradict Victor. And anyway, Blossom have she desires and Victor have more than reputation between he legs.

So life go on as it supposed to go on, until Blossom decide not to go to work one day. That time, they was living on Vaughan Road and Blossom wake up feeling like a old woman. Just tired. Something tell she to stay home and figure out she life, because a thirty-six-year-old woman shouldn't feel so old and tired. She look at she face in the mirror and figure that she look like a old woman too. Ten years she here now, and nothing shaking, just getting older and older, watching white people live. She, sheself living underneath all the time. She didn't even feel like living with Victor anymore. All the sugar gone outa the thing. Victor had one scheme after another, poor thing. Everything gone a little sour.

She was looking out the window, toward the bus stop on Vaughan Road, thinking this. Looking at people going to work like they does do every morning. It make she even more tired to watch them. Today she was supposed to go to a house on Roselawn. Three bathrooms to clean, two living rooms, basement, laundry — God knows what else. Fifty dollars. She look at she short fingers, still water-laden from the day before, then look at the bus stop again. No, no. Not today. Not this woman. In the bedroom, she watch Victor lying in the bed, face peaceful as ever, young like a baby. Passing into the kitchen shaking she head, she think, "Victor, you ain't ready for the Lord yet."

Blossom must be was sitting at the kitchen table for a hour or so when Victor get up. She hear him bathe, dress, and come out to the kitchen. "Ah, ah, you still here? Is ten o'clock you know!" She didn't answer. "Girl, you ain't going to work today, or what?" She didn't answer. "You is a happy woman yes, Blossom. Anyway," as he put he coat on, "I have to meet a fella." Something just fly up in Blossom head and she reach for the bread knife on the table. "Victor, just go and don't come back, you hear me?"

waving the knife. "Girl you crazy, or what?" Victor edged toward the door, "What happen to you this morning?"

Next thing Blosom know, she running Victor down Vaughan Road screaming and waving the bread knife. She hear somebody screaming loud, loud. At first she didn't know who it is, and is then she realize that the scream was coming from she and she couldn't stop it. She dress in she nightie alone and screaming in the middle of the road. So it went on and on and on until it turn into cry and Blossom just cry and cry and cry and then she start to walk. That day Blossom walk. And walk and cry, until she was so exhausted that she find she way home and went to sleep.

She wake up the next morning, feeling shaky and something like spiritual. She was frightened, in case the crying come back again. The apartment was empty. She had the feeling that she was holding she body around she heart, holding sheself together, tight, tight. She get dressed and went to the Pentecostal Church where she get married and sit there till evening.

For two weeks this is all Blossom do. As soon as she feel the crying welling up inside she and turning to a scream, she get dressed and go to the Pentecost. After two weeks, another feeling come; one as if Blossom dip she whole head in water and come up gasping. She heart would pump fast as if she going to die and then the feeling, washed and gasping. During these weeks she could drink nothing but water. When she try to eat bread, something reach inside of she throat and spit it out. Two weeks more and Blossom hair turn white all over. Then she start to speak in tongues that she didn't ever learn, but she understand. At night, in Blossom cry dreams, she feel sheself flying round the earth and raging around the world and then, not just this earth, but earth deep in the blackness beyond sky. There, sky become further than sky and further than dream. She dream so much farther than she ever go in a dream, that she was awake. Blossom see volcano erupt and mountain fall down two feet away and she ain't get touch. She come to the place where *legahoo* and *lajabless* is not even dog and where *soucouyant*, the fireball, burn up in the bigger fire of an infinite sun, where none of the ordinary spirit Blossom know is nothing. She come to the place where pestilence mount good, good heart and good heart bust for joy. The place bright one minute and dark the next. The place big one minute, so big Blossom standing in a hole and the blackness rising up like long shafts above she and widening out into a yellow and red desert as far as she could see; the place small, next minute, as a pin head and only Blossom heart what shrink small, small, small, could fit in the world of it. Then she feel as if she don't have no hand, no foot, and she don't need them. Sometimes, she crawling like a mapeepee snake; sometimes she walking tall, tall, like a *moco jumbie* through desert and darkness, desert and darkness, upside down and sideways.

In the mornings, Blossom feel she body beating up and breaking up on a hard mud ground and she, weeping as if she mourning and as if somebody borning. And talking in tongues, the tongues saying the name, Oya. The name sound through Blossom into every layer of she skin, she flesh — like sugar and seasoning. Blossom body come hard like steel and supple like water when she say Oya. Oya. This Oya was a big spirit Blossom know from home.

One night, Oya hold Blossom and bring she through the most terrifying dream in she life. In the dream, Oya make Blossom look at Black people suffering. The face of Black people suffering was so old and hoary that Blossom nearly dead. And is so she vomit. She skin wither under Suffering look; and she feel hungry and thirsty as nobody ever feel before. Pain dry out Blossom soul, until it turn to nothing. Blossom so 'fraid she dead that she take she last ball of spit, and stone Suffering. Suffering jump up so fast and grab the stone, Blossom shocked, because she did think Suffering was decrepit. Then Suffering head for Blossom with such a speed that Blossom fingernails and hairs fall out. Blossom start to dry away, and melt away, until it only had one grain of she left. And Suffering still descending. Blossom scream for Oya and Oya didn't come and Suffering keep coming. Blossom was never a woman to stop, even before she start to dream. So she roll and dance she grain-self into a hate so hard, she chisel sheself into a sharp, hot prickle and fly in Suffering face. Suffering howl like a beast and back back. Blossom spin and chew on that nut of hate, right in Suffering eyeball. The more Blossom spin and dance, the more Suffering back back; the more Suffering back back, the bigger Blossom get, until Blossom was Oya with she warrior knife, advancing. In the cold light of Suffering, with Oya hot and advancing, Suffering slam a door and disappear. Blossom climb into Oya lovely womb of strength and fearlessness. Full of joy when Oya show she the warrior dance where heart and blood burst open. Freeness, Oya call that dance; and the colour of the dance was red and it was a dance to dance high up in the air. In this dance Oya had such a sweet laugh, it make she black skin shake and it full up Blossom and shake she too.

Each night Blossom grow more into Oya. Blossom singing, singing for Oya to come,

"*Oya arriwo Oya, Oya arriwo Oya, Oya kauako arriwo, Arripiti O Oya.*"

Each night Blossom learn a new piece of Oya and finally, it come to she. She had the power to see and the power to fight; she had the power to feel pain and the power to heal. For life was nothing as it could be taken away any minute;

what was earthy was fleeting. What could be done was joy and it have no beauty in suffering. *"Oya O Ologbo O de, Ma yak ba Ma Who! Oya O Ologo O de, Ma yak ba Ma Who! leh, Oya Oh de arriwo, Oya Oh de crumale."* From that day, Blossom dress in yellow and red from head to foot, the colour of joy and the colour of war against suffering. She head wrap in a long yellow cloth; she body wrap in red. She become a obeah woman, spiritual mother and priestess of Oya, Yuroba Goddess-warrior of winds, storms and waterfalls. It was Oya who run Victor out and it was Oya who plague the doctor and laugh and drink afterwards. It was Oya who well up the tears inside Blossom and who spit the bread out of Blossom mouth.

Quite here, Oya did search for Blossom. Quite here, she find she.

Black people on Vaughan Road recognized Blossom as gifted and powerful by she carriage and the fierce look in she eyes. She fill she rooms with compelling powder and reliance smoke, drink rum and spit it in the corners, for the spirits who would enter Blossom obeah house in the night. Little by little people begin to find out that Blossom was the priestess of Oya, the Goddess. Is through Oya, that Blossom reach prosperity.

"Oya arriwo Oya, Oya arriwo Oya, Oya kauako arriwo, Arripita O Oya."

Each night Oya would enter Blossom, rumbling and violent like thunder and chant heroically and dance, slowly and majestically, she warrior dance against suffering. To see Oya dancing on one leg all night, a calabash holding a candle on she head, was to see beauty. She fierce warrior face frighten unbelievers. Then she would drink nothing but good liquor, blowing mouthfuls on the gathering, granting favours to the believers for an offering.

41

The offerings come fast and plentiful. Where people was desperate, Blossom, as Oya, received food as offering, boxes of candles and sweet oil. Blossom send to Trinidad for calabash gourds and herbs for healing, guided by Oya in the mixing and administering.

When Oya enter Blosssom, she talk in old African tongues and she body was part water and part tree. Oya thrash about taking Blossom body up to the ceiling and right through the walls. Oya knife slash the gullets of white men and Oya pitch the world around itself. Some nights, she voice sound as if it was coming from a deep well; and some nights, only if you had the power to hear air, could you listen to Oya.

Blossom fame as a obeah woman spread all over, but only among those who had to know. Those who see the hoary face of Suffering and feel he vibrant slap could come to dance with Oya — Oya freeness dance.

"Oya O Ologbo O de, Ma yak ba Ma Who! leh, Oya O Ologo O de, Ma yak ba Ma Who! leh, Oya Oh de arriwo, Oya Oh de cumale."

Since Oya reach, Blossom live peaceful. Is so, Blossom start in the speakeasy business. In the day time, Blossom sleep, exhausted and full of Oya warrior dance and laughing. She would wake up in the afternoon to prepare the shrine for Oya entrance.

On the nights that Oya didn't come, Blossom sell liquor and wait for she, sitting against the window.

St. Mary's Estate

St. Mary's Estate was further on. Past the two rum and grocery shops, past Miss Dot's, past the savannah, past Miss Jeanne's parlour — paradise plums in large bottle jars. Then a piece of bush. Then St. Mary's.

Most of it is still there I notice, as the jeep misses the St. Mary's entrance and drives a little way on to Schoener's Road, the dried-out river bed in which duennes used to play all night, or so the story goes. I tell my sister this is where the spirits of dead unchristened children used to live, *duennes,* calling children in the evening to come and play. Our friend, driving the jeep, asks if I want to write down the correct spelling of the name of the road. I tell him it does not matter. I have known that road and that dry river bed for thirty-four years with a mixture of fear and curiosity, though I've only ever stood this distance from it. The story might still be true. The trees and the stones have been preserved in my head with their sign of silence, yellowness, and eerie emptiness. When we look toward the river bed, the three of us, we look as if we're watching something or someone. Not emigration, not schooling, not brightly lit cities have managed to remove the shapes of duennes in the river bed by Schoener's Road. Not even Schoener, probably a dutch privateer, with all his greed and wickedness, debauchery and woman-burning, not even he could remove the shapes of duennes in this river bed, by putting his strange name to it. It is still quiet, waiting for dusk for duennes to come out calling to play whoop.

The jeep turns around. The two male passengers of a truck leaving Schoener's Road stare at us as the vehicles negotiate passage. Then the jeep turns right into the gravelled entrance of St. Mary's. There is still a white signboard on a post, now leaning into the ditch at the entrance, now wood-lice eaten. The letters are worn, but officious and distant; painted a long time ago, they survive like the post. A vigilant reminder and a current record of ownership and property. At this point you can see the sea straight ahead, in back of the house where I was born. This entrance gives you a sense of coming home, the same sense I've always had upon seeing it. The eyes light on the completeness of the scene it guards. There are two long barracks, one on each side of the gravel road. In front of the right barracks there is a great tamarind tree, now a little shrivelled but still protecting the place underneath, dirt swept clean, where people, mostly men, used to gather and play cards, drink rum, and talk. Of the two barracks, this one still houses people. All that is left of the other are the nine-to-twelve thick white pillars which it stood on once and the triangular moving roof under which copra is put to dry. Bush has overgrown the floors and the walls have been removed, perhaps from fire, or perhaps from ancient wear, sunk into the ground. That's where Cousin Johnny used to live. He was deaf and did not speak. He made beautiful soups and mouth-watering coconut bakes and saltfish. The whole compound would smell sweetly of his bakes on a Saturday evening.

The jeep eases along for another fifty yards; my eyes rest on the place, old and familiar like watching the past, feeling comfortable and awestruck at once. Then, too, resentful and sad. A boy atop the left barracks stops raking the copra to watch us. No one else is about. The air is very still, yet breathing, a breeze, quiet and fresh, blowing from the sea. The sea here, too, is still. A country beach, a beach for scavenging children, thinking women, fishermen. The sea is not rough or fantastic, nothing more stupendous than an ordinary beauty, ever rolling, ever present. The kind of sea to raise your eyes to from labour. This must have been the look toward the sea that slaves saw as they pulled oxen, cut and shelled coconut, dug provisions from the black soil on the north side of the road. This must have been a look of envy.

There used to be a big well near the tamarind tree. Plait Hair and Tamasine used to live over there, in the third place of the back row of the right barracks. She had seventeen children; he plaited his hair, refusing to cut it. He worked hard, always in silence, his cheeks sucked in. Tamasine was a big red woman, as big as Plait Hair was slight and wiry. The walls separating each quarter of the barracks from the other did not go up to the roof, so everyone could hear what was going on in the other. Each quarter was one room. People used to wonder how Plait Hair and Tamasine had seventeen children, since it was difficult to be private. Maybe they'd wait till everyone was asleep, including their children. Even now, I find myself speculating.

There used to be a lagoon on the left, past the left barracks, off into the bush. . . .

The gravel road slows the jeep, as it edges toward the small wood house where I was born. Set in the centre to observe the two barracks, its back is toward the sea, its legs standing halfway in sand, halfway in dirt. It's the same house, thirty-four years later. The jeep moves even more slowly because of the silence of the place. As it passes the barracks there is no sign or sound of life except the boy on the copra house gone back to his work.

"It's the same house," I say, and to my sister, "Do you remember it?"

"No," she says, "I wasn't born yet."

Two men come out of the house as the jeep pulls to a stop near the front steps. I recognize one of them as the man who took over after my grandfather was fired as overseer of St. Mary's Estate. An emotion like resentfulness rises in me. It is only a memory of my grandfather, in his sixties; after twenty years, he was to be let go and, from what I could pick up at three or four-years old, this new man was the cause. The new man, the overseer, is now an old man. His youth had been thrown in my grandfather's face and his ability to husband cocoa. I'm amused that something learned such a long time ago can still call upon the same emotion and have it come, fresh and sharp like this. I put on a smile and walk up the steps, my hand outstretched, saying, "Hi, I was born in this house. I just want to look around." He cracks a smile in his stern face, as recognition passes over his eyes and confirms, "Oh, you is a Jordann," saying my last name as it has always sounded — like the name of a tribe, a set of characteristics ranging criminal to saint, axe women to shango priestess, obeah woman. My grandfather's life put the sound into my last name. My grandmother's life put the silence after it. *Jordann,* like a bearing, like a drum.

My grandfather had children and outside women and outside children. He could read and he could write, which made him valuable. He was the overseer for twenty years at

St. Mary's. He had an ornate hand and was such a strict parent that all his children wrote exactly like him. He rode two horses, Noble and Buddha. Noble was white and Buddha was black. Noble for show and Buddha for faithfulness. He drank rum at the first shop and the second shop, drinking and gambling out the pittance that he made tending St. Mary's for a white man. He wrote letters and took care of everyone else's business. He gave advice freely; he took only advice which could ruin him. He always walked straight up and stiff, the length of his six feet. Until the last years which he spent here, he lived a life of grace, depending on what was not possible, riches, and escaping payment of the debts he incurred dreaming about it. Grace only lasts forever with God, not with white men, so papa was disposed of when age was tired of holding out on his face and when he was unable to create a vision of acres of rich purple cocoa trees for the estate owner. Then everything caught up with him, mostly his debts, and we all went to live in town, except he.

He first went to live in a house up a steep cliff which he could not mount because of his sore foot and then settled into a shack near the road where he sold ground provisions — callaloo bush, okra, and pepper. Finally he got a job as an agricultural officer, walking miles into the bush to talk to farmers. The last entries in his diary, the ones before he died, only said, optimistically, "Can't go to work, sick today."

The dirt around the house is mixed with sand and broken bits of shells. During deep tide, the sea comes in as far as the front yard, lashing against the pillow tree trunks which the house stands atop. We get the okay from the new man and head toward the beach. My sister and our friend follow me as I tell them,

"There used to be a lagoon over there; once it caught on

fire. This is where we used to put garbage. See the shells are better here. This is a place for a kid to hunt shells and stones. This is where I used to play."

They follow me, looking at me a little strangely or perhaps trying to see what I see. My childhood — hunting up and down the beach for shells, stones, bits of bottles, snails, things washed up by the sea, lagan; the blue-red transparent shine of *garlent*; seeing how far you could walk; pointing to Point Galeoto; swearing we could see Venezuela; digging into crab holes.

"This is a place for a kid," I say. "Every Good Friday, a tree would appear in the lagoon. Mama said it was a sign of Christ."

We move away toward the lagoon. It is the dry season. The lagoon is still there despite the years of garbage throwing. Then we walk back toward the house, along the beach, and I point toward a river's mouth rippling into the sea, two hundred yards to the right of the wooden house.

"It was hard to cross there, the tide was too strong sometimes."

And then I see it, and I feel something in me hesitate to walk toward that side. It is a huge green house, hidden from the wood house by trees, but visible on the sea side. It used to be yellow, it seems to me; but I could be mistaken. Rust, brought on by the spray of the sea, swells on its sides. It is empty and it is closed. I turn to my sister,

"That fucking house. Do you see that fucking house!"

My sister looks at me, understanding. I cannot bring myself to move toward the house or that part of the beach.

"That goddamned house. It's still there."

I feel such anger and yet, still, my feet do not move toward it. So angry, I feel nauseous. "Fuckers!" I yell, but the wind and the sound of the sea lift the word and balloon it into a feeble scream. The uselessness of that sound stops me, and I explain to our friend who looks perturbed, "That's where they used to live."

In fact, they didn't live there. They came with their children every July. Then we had to be reverential toward them; we could not walk to that side, especially if they were on the beach. They left at the end of August and then we kids would rush, with my mama who went to clean the house, to see what they had left. Even what they had left we could not touch, thank God, because mama wouldn't allow us. Mostly, we children envied the real doll's head that lay here or there and the shoes discarded. Their children always wore shoes and socks. We ran about like mad things in bare feet and washed-out clothing.

For two months, this wasn't our place. For two months papa bowed and scraped, visibly. And mama warned us grandchildren not to misbehave or embarrass the family.

And still after this long, the imperative of habit and station causes my legs to stand where they are. Do not go near the house. It is the white people's house. It is their place and we are "niggers." Reaching back into me, thirty-four years, a command, visceral, fresh as the first day it was given. It still had the power of starvation, whip and . . . blood. I turn and we walk back toward the wood house and the stern-faced new man.

This is where I was born. This is the white people's house. This is the overseer's shack. Those are the estate workers' barracks. This is where I was born. That is the white people's house this is the overseer's shack those are the slave barracks. That is the slave owner's house this is the overseer's shack those are the slave barracks.

This estate has been here for hundreds of years. Papa was the overseer. It is the end of the twentieth century and the slave barracks are still standing; one, with people living in it; the other refusing to drop into the earth, even though it has no walls. Tamasine and Plait Hair used to live in the barracks, Uncle Johnny used to live in the one that's half gone. The walls were thin cardboard and the daily gazette was used as wallpaper.

To sleep beneath the raw stench of copra, night after night, for two hundred years is not easy; to hear tired breathing, breathless fucking, children screaming for five hundred years is not easy. And the big house was always empty, except for two months of the year. The slave barracks whose layers of gazette paper stretched for hundreds of years, was packed with Black humanity, rolling over and over and over without end, and still. This is where I was born. This is how I know struggle, know it like a landscaper. An artist could not have drawn it better.

"Fuckers. Fuckers. Fuckers." I hear myself muttering, under my breath. "Fu-u-ck, they're still there."

I go up the steps of the wood house, asking the new man,

"Sir, who owns this place?"

"Hackens and them, nah,' he replies, leaning his now gray head as if I should know or remember, "They always own it."

"Always?"

"Yes." The new man nods as he speaks, "You know, them is big shot."

I must not have remembered about the house because now I can see it from the front of the wood house, too. Twenty of us were born in the two rooms of this wood house, while that one stood empty, locked. I'm looking to where I had instinctively not looked before. The house is still there, green, the windows locked, rust bleeding from its joints.

We climb into the jeep saying good-bye to the new man.

Always.

The jeep hobbles up the gravel road past the quiet barracks. The boy on the roof doesn't stop his work this time to look at us. We get to the sign post. "St. Mary's Estate," it says once again, judiciously. Red-eyed, I have a picture of the green house in my head, ablaze.

Photograph

My grandmother has left no trace, no sign of her self. There is no photograph, except one which she took with much trouble for her identity card. I remember the day that she had to take it. It was for voting, when we got Independence; and my grandmother, with fear in her eyes, woke up that morning, got dressed, put on her hat, and left. It was the small beige hat with the lace piece for the face. There was apprehension in the house. My grandmother, on these occasions, the rare ones when she left the house, patted her temples with limacol. Her smelling salts were placed in her purse. The little bottle with the green crystals and liquid had a pungent odour and a powerful aura for me until I was much older. She never let us touch it. She kept it in her purse, now held tightly in one hand, the same hand which held her one embroidered handkerchief.

That morning we all woke up and were put to work getting my grandmother ready to go to the identity card place.

One of us put the water to boil for my grandmother's bath. My big sister combed her hair, and the rest of us were dispatched to get shoes, petticoat, or stockings. My grand-mother's mouth moved nervously as these events took place and her fingers hardened over ours each time our clumsy efforts crinkled a pleat or spilled scent.

We were an ever-growing bunch of cousins, sisters, and brothers. My grandmother's grandchildren. Children of my grandmother's daughters. We were seven in all, from time to time more, given to my grandmother for safekeeping. Eula, Kat, Ava, and I were sisters. Eula was the oldest. Genevieve, Wil, and Dri were sister and brothers and our cousins. Our mothers were away. Away-away or in the country-away. That's all we knew of them except for their photographs which we used tauntingly in our battles about whose mother was prettier.

Like the bottle of smelling salts, all my grandmother's things had that same aura. We would wait until she was out of sight, which only meant that she was in the kitchen since she never left the house, and then we would try on her dresses or her hat, or open the bottom drawer of the wardrobe where she kept sheets, pillowcases, and underwear, candles and candlesticks, boxes of matches, pieces of cloth for headties and dresses and curtains, black cake and wafers, rice and sweet bread, in pillowcases, just in case of an emergency. We would unpack my grand-mother's things down to the bottom of the drawer, where she kept camphor balls, and touch them over and over again. We would wrap ourselves in pieces of cloth, pretending we were African queens; we would put on my grandmother's gold chain, pretending we were rich. We would pinch her black cakes until they were down to nothing and then we would swear that we never touched them and never saw who did. Often, she caught us and beat us, but we were always on the lookout for the next chance to interfere in my grandmother's sacred things.

There was always something new there. Once, just before Christmas, we found a black doll. It caused commotion and rare dissension among us. All of us wanted it, so, of course, my grandmother discovered us. None of us, my grandmother said, deserved it and on top of that she threatened that there would be no Santa Claus for us. She kept the doll at the head of her bed until she relented and gave it to Kat, who was the littlest.

We never knew how anything got into the drawer because we never saw things enter the house. Everything in the drawer was pressed and ironed and smelled of starch and ironing and newness and oldness. My grandmother guarded them often more like burden than treasure. Their depletion would make her anxious; their addition would pose problems of space in our tiny house.

As she rarely left the house, my grandmother felt that everyone on the street where we lived would be looking at her, going to take her picture for her identity card. We felt the same, too, and worried as she left, stepping heavily yet shakily down the short hill that lead to the savannah, at the far end of which was the community centre. My big sister held her hand. We could see the curtains moving discreetly in the houses next to ours as my grandmother walked, head up, face hidden behind her veil. We prayed that she would not fall. She had warned us not to hang out of the windows looking at her. We, nevertheless, hung out of the windows gawking at her, along with the woman who lived across the street, whom my grandmother thought lived a scandalous life and had scandalous children and a scandalous laugh which could be heard all the way up the street when the woman sat old blagging with her friends on her veranda. We now hung out of the windows keeping company with Tante, as she was called, standing with her hands on her massive hips looking and praying for my grandmother. She did not stop, nor did she turn back to give us her look. But we knew that the minute she returned our ears would be burning because we had joined Tante in disgracing my grandmother.

The photograph from that outing is the only one we have of my grandmother, and it is all wrinkled and chewed up, even after my grandmother hid it from us and warned us not to touch it. Someone retrieved it when my grandmother was taken to the hospital. The laminate was now dull, and my grandmother's picture was gray and creased and distant.

As my grandmother turned the corner with my sister, the rest of us turned to lawlessness, eating sugar from the kitchen and opening the new refrigerator as often as we wanted and rummaging through my grandmother's things. Dressed up in my grandmother's clothes and splashing each other with her limacol, we paraded outside the house where she had distinctly told us not to go. We waved at Tante, mincing along in my grandmother's shoes. After a while, we grew tired and querulous; assessing the damage we had done to the kitchen, the sugar bowl, and my grandmother's wardrobe, we began assigning blame. We all decided to tell on each other. Who had more sugar than whom and who was the first to open the cabinet drawer where my grandmother kept our birth certificates.

We liked to smell our birth certificates. Their musty smell and yellowing water-marked coarse paper was proof that my grandmother owned us. She had made such a fuss to get them from our mothers.

A glum silence descended when we realized that it was useless quarrelling. We were all implicated and my grandmother always beat everyone, no matter who committed the crime.

When my grandmother returned we were too chas-

tened to protest her beating. We began to cry as soon as we
saw her coming around the corner with my sister. By the
time she hit the doorstep we were weeping buckets and
the noise we made sounded like a wake, groaning in
unison and holding onto each other. My grandmother, too
tired from her ordeal at the identity card place, looked at
us scornfully and sat down. There was a weakness in her
eyes which we recognized. It meant that our beating
would be postponed for hours, maybe days, until she
could regain her strength. She had been what seemed like
hours at the identity card place. My grandmother had to
wait, leaning on my sister and having people stare at her,
she said. All that indignity, and the pain which always
appeared in her back at these moments, had made her
barely able to walk back to the house. We, too, had been so
distraught that we did not even stand outside the house
jumping up and down and shouting that she was coming.
So at least she was spared that embarrassment. For the rest
of the day we quietly went about our chores, without being
told to do them, and walked lightly past my grandmother's
room, where she lay resting in a mound, under the pink
chenille.

We had always lived with my grandmother. None of
us could recollect our mothers, except as letters from
England or occasional visits from women who came on
weekends and made plans to take us, eventually, to live
with them. The letters from England came every two
weeks and at Christmas with a brown box full of foreign-
smelling clothes. The clothes smelled of a good life in a
country where white people lived and where bad-behaved
children like us would not be tolerated. All this my grandmother said. There, children had manners and didn't play
in mud and didn't dirty everything and didn't cry if there
wasn't any food and didn't run under the mango trees,

grabbing mangoes when the wind blew them down and walked and did not run through the house like *warrahoons* and did not act like little old *niggers.* Eula, my big sister, would read the letters to my grandmother who, from time to time, would let us listen. Then my grandmother would urge us to grow up and go away too and live well. When she came to the part about going away, we would feel half-proud and half-nervous. The occasional visits made us feel as precarious as the letters. When we misbehaved, my grandmother often threatened to send us away-away, where white men ate Black children, or to quite-too-quite in the country.

Passing by my grandmother's room, bunched up under the spread, with her face tight and hollow-cheeked, her mouth set against us, the spectre of quite-to-quite and white cannibals loomed brightly. It was useless trying to "dog back" to her, she said, when one of my cousins sat close to her bed, inquiring if she would like us to pick her gray hairs out. That was how serious this incident was. Because my grandmother loved us to pick her gray hairs from her head. She would promise us a penny for every ten which we could get by the root. If we broke a hair, that would not count, she said. And, if we threw the little balls of her hair out into the yard for the wind, my grandmother became quite upset since that meant that birds would fly off with her hair and send her mad, send her mind to the four corners of the earth, or they would build a nest with her hair and steal her brain. We never threw hair in the yard for the wind, at least not my grandmother's hair, and we took on her indignant look when we chastised each other for doing it with our own hair. My cousin Genevieve didn't mind though. She chewed her long front plait when she sucked on her thumb and saved balls of hair to throw to the birds. Genevieve made mudpies under the house, which we bought with leaf money. You could get yellow mudpies or brown mudpies or red mudpies. This depended on the depth of the hole under the house and the wash water which my grandmother threw there on Saturdays. We took my grandmother's word that having to search the four corners of the earth for your mind was not an easy task, but Genevieve wondered what it would be like.

There's a photograph of Genevieve and me and two of my sisters someplace. We took it to send to England. My grandmother dressed us up, put my big sister in charge of us, giving her 50 cents tied up in a handkerchief and pinned to the waistband of her dress, and warned us not to give her any trouble. We marched to Wong's Studio on the Coffee, the main road in our town, and fidgeted as Mr. Wong fixed us in front of a promenade scene to take our picture. My little sister cried through it all and sucked her fingers. Nobody knows that it's me in the photograph, but my sisters and Genevieve look like themselves.

Banishment from my grandmother's room was torture. It was her room, even though three of us slept beside her each night. It was a small room with two windows kept shut most of the time, except every afternoon when my grandmother would look out of the front window, her head resting on her big arms, waiting for us to return from school. There was a bed in the room with a headboard where she kept the bible, a bureau with a round mirror, and a washstand with a jug and basin. She spent much of her time here. We, too, sitting on the polished floor under the front window talking to her or against the foot of the bed, if we were trying to get back into her favour or beg her for money. We knew the smell of the brown varnished wood of her bed intimately.

My grandmother's room was rescue from pursuit. Anyone trying to catch anyone would pull up straight and get quiet, if you ducked into her room. We read under my grandmother's bed and, playing catch, we hid from each other behind the bulk of her body.

We never received that licking for the photograph day, but my grandmother could keep a silence that was punishment enough. The photograph now does not look like her. It is gray and pained. In real, she was round and comfortable. When we knew her she had a full lap and beautiful arms; her cocoa brown skin smelled of wood smoke and familiar.

My grandmother never thought that people should sleep on Saturdays. She woke us up *peepee au jour,* as she called it, which meant before it was light outside, and set us to work. My grandmother said that she couldn't stand a lazy house, full of lazy children. The washing had to be done and dried before three o'clock on Saturday when the baking would begin and continue until the evening. My big sister and my grandmother did the washing, leaning over the scrubbing board and the tub, and when we others grew older we scrubbed the clothes out, under the eyes of my grandmother. We had to lay the soap-scrubbed clothes out on the square pile of stones so that the sun would bleach them clean, then pick them up and rinse and hang them to dry. We all learned to bake from the time that our chins could reach the table, and we washed dishes standing on the bench in front of the sink. In the rainy season, the washing was done on the sunniest days. A sudden shower of rain and my grandmother would send us flying to collect the washing off the lines. We would sit for hours watching the rain gush through the drains which we had dug, in anticipation, around the flower garden in front of the house. The yellow-brown water lumbered unsteadily through the drains rebuilding the mud and forming a lake at the place where our efforts were frustrated by a large stone.

In the rainy season, my big sister planted corn and pigeon peas on the right side of the house. Just at the tail end of the season, we planted the flower garden. Zinnias and jump-up-and-kiss-me, which grew easily, and xora and roses, which we could never get to grow. Only the soil on one side of the front yard was good for growing flowers or food. On the other side a sour-sop tree and an almond tree sucked the soil of everything, leaving the ground sandy and thin, and pushed up their roots, ridging the yard into a hill. The almond tree, under the front window, fed a nest of ants which lived in one pillar of our house. A line of small red ants could be seen making their way from pillar to almond tree, carrying bits of leaves and bark.

One Saturday evening, I tried to stay outside playing longer than allowed by my grandmother, leaning on the almond tree and ignoring her calls. "Laugh and cry live in the same house," my grandmother warned, threatening to beat me when I finally came inside. At first I only felt the bite of one ant on my leg but, no sooner, my whole body was invaded by thousands of little red ants biting my skin blue crimson. My sisters and cousins laughed, my grandmother, looking at me pitiably, sent me to the shower; but the itching did not stop and the pains did not subside until the next day.

I often polished the floor on Saturdays. At first, I hated the brown polish-dried rag with which I had to rub the floors, creeping on my hands and knees. I hated the corners of the room which collected fluff and dust. If we tried to polish the floor without first scrubbing it, my grandmother would make us start all over again. My grandmother supervised all these activities when she was ill, sitting on the bed. She saw my distaste for the rag and therefore insisted that I polish over and over again some spot which I was sure that I had gone over. I learned to look at the rag, to notice its layers of brown polish, its waxy shine in some places, its wetness when my grandmother made me mix the polish with kerosene to stretch its use. It became a rich object, all full of continuous ribbing and working, which my grandmother insisted that I do with my hands and no shortcuts of standing and doing it with the heel of my foot. We poor people had to get used to work, my grandmother said. After polishing, we would shine the floor with more rags. Up and down, until my grandmother was satisfied. Then the morris chairs, whose slats fell off every once in a while with our jumping, had to be polished and shined, and the cabinet, and all put back in their place.

She wasted nothing. Everything turned into something else when it was too old to be everything. Dresses turned into skirts and then into underwear. Shoes turned into slippers. Corn, too hard for eating, turned into meal. My grandmother herself never wore anything new, except when she went out. She had two dresses and a petticoat hanging in the wardrobe for those times. At home, she dressed in layers of old clothing, half-slip over dress, old socks, because her feet were always cold, and slippers, cut out of old shoes. A safety pin or two, anchored to the front of her dress or the hem of her skirt, to pin up our falling underwear or ruined zippers.

My grandmother didn't like it when we changed the furniture around. She said that changing the furniture around was a sign to people that we didn't have any money. Only people with no money changed their furniture around and around all the time. My grandmother had various lectures on money, to protect us from the knowledge that we had little or none. At night, we could not drop pennies on the floor, for thieves might be passing and think that we did have money and come to rob us.

My grandmother always said that money ran through your hands like water, especially when you had so many mouths to feed. Every two or three weeks money would run out of my grandmother's hands. These times were as routine as our chores or going to school or the games which we played. My grandmother had stretched it over stewed chicken, rice, provisions, and macaroni pie on Sundays, split peas soup on Mondays, fish and bake on Tuesdays, corn meal dumplings and salt cod on Wednesdays, okra and rice on Thursdays, split peas, salt cod, and rice on Fridays, and pelau on Saturdays. By the time the third week of the month came around my grandmother's stretching would become apparent. She carried a worried look on her face and was more silent than usual. We understood this to be a sign of lean times and times when we could not bother my grandmother or else we would get one of her painful explanations across our ears. Besides it really hurt my grandmother not to give us what we needed, as we all settled with her into a depressive hungry silence.

At times we couldn't help but look accusingly at her. Who else could we blame for the gnawing pain in our stomachs and the dry corners of our mouths. We stared at my grandmother hungrily, while she avoided our eyes. We would all gather around her as she lay in bed, leaning against her or sitting on the floor beside the bed, all in silence. We devoted these silences to hope — hope that something would appear to deliver us, perhaps my grandfather, with provisons from the country — and to wild imagination that we would be rich some day and be able to buy pounds of sugar and milk. But sweet water, a thin mixture of water and sugar, was all the balm for our hunger. When even that did not show itself in abundance, our silences were even deeper. We drank water, until our stomachs became distended and nautical.

My little sister, who came along a few years after we had grown accustomed to the routine of hunger and silence, could never grasp the importance of these moments. We made her swear not to cry for food when there wasn't any and, to give her credit, she did mean it when she promised. But the moment the hungry silence set in, she began to cry, begging my grandmother for sweet water. She probably cried out of fear that we would never eat again, and admittedly our silences were somewhat awesome, mixtures of despair and grief made potent by the weakness which the heavy, hot sun brought on in our bodies.

We resented my little sister for these indiscretions. She reminded us that we were hungry, a thought we had been transcending in our growing asceticism, and we felt sorry for my grandmother having to answer her cries. Because it was only then that my grandmother relented and sent one of us to borrow a cup of sugar from the woman across the street. One of us suffered the indignity of crossing the road and repeating haltingly whatever words my grandmother had told her to say.

My grandmother always sent us to Tante, never to Mrs. Sommard who was a religious woman and our next-door neighbour, nor to Mrs. Benjamin who had money and was our other next-door neighbour. Mrs. Sommard only had prayers to give and Mrs.Benjamin, scorn. But Tante, with nothing, like us, would give whatever she could manage. Mrs. Sommard was a Seventh Day Adventist, and the only time my grandmother sent one of us to beg a cup of something, Mrs. Sommard sent back a message to pray. My grandmother took it quietly and never sent us there again and told us to have respect for Mrs. Sommard because she

was a religious woman and believed that God would pro-
vide.

Mrs. Sommard's husband, Mr. Sommard, took two years
to die. For the two years that he took to die the house was
always brightly lit. Mr. Sommard was so afraid of dying
that he could not sleep and didn't like it when darkness
fell. He stayed awake all night and all day for two years and
kept his wife and daughter awake too. My grandmother
said he pinched them if they fell asleep and told them that
if he couldn't sleep, they shouldn't sleep either. How this
ordeal squared with Mrs. Sommard's religiousness, my
grandmother was of two minds about. Either the Lord was
trying Mrs. Sommard's faith, or Mrs. Sommard had done
some wickedness that the Lord was punishing her for.

The Benjamins, on the the other side, we didn't know
where they got their money from, but they seemed to have
a lot of it. For Mrs. Benjamin sometimes told our friend
Patsy not to play with us. Patsy lived with Mrs. Benjamin,
her grandmother; Miss Lena, her aunt, and her grandfather,
Mr. Benjamin. We could always smell chicken that Miss
Lena was cooking from their pot, even when our house fell
into silence.

The Benjamins were the reason that my grandmother
didn't like us running down into the backyard to pick up
mangoes when the wind blew them down. She felt a-
shamed that we would show such hunger in the eyes of
people who had plenty. The next thing was that the
Benjamins' rose mango tree was so huge, it spread half its
body over their fence into our yard. We felt that this meant
that any mangoes that dropped on our side belonged to us,
and Patsy Benjamin and her family thought that it belonged to them. My grandmother took their side, not
because she thought that they were right, but she thought
that if they were such greedy people, they should have the

mangoes. Let them kill themselves on it, she said. So she made us call to Mrs. Benjamin and give them all the rose mangoes that fell in our yard. Mrs. Benjamin thought that we were doing this out of respect for their status and so she would often tell us with superiority to keep the mangoes, but my grandmother would decline. We, grudgingly, had to do the same and, as my grandmother warned us, without a sad look on our faces. From time to time we undermined my grandmother's pride by pretending not to find any rose mangoes on the ground, and hid them in a stash under the house or deep in the backyard under leaves. Since my grandmother never ventured from the cover and secrecy of the walls of the house, or that area in the yard hidden by the walls, she was never likely to discover our lie.

Deep in the backyard, over the drain which we called the canal, we were out of range of my grandmother's voice, since she refused to shout, and the palms of her hands, but not her eyes. We were out of reach of her broomstick which she flung at our fleeing backs or up into one of the mango trees where one of us was perched, escaping her beatings.

Deep in the back of the yard, we smoked sponge wood and danced in risqué fashion and uttered the few cuss words that we knew and made up calypsos. There, we pretended to be big people with children. We put our hands on our hips and shook our heads, as we had seen big people do, and complained about having so much children, children, children to feed.

My grandmother showed us how to kill a chicken, holding its body in the tub and placing the scrubbing board over it leaving the neck exposed, then with a sharp knife quickly cut the neck, leaving the scrubbing board over the tub. Few of us became expert at killing a chicken.

The beating of the dying fowl would frighten us and the scrubbing board would slip whereupon the headless bird would escape, its warm blood still gushing, propelling its body around and around the house. My grandmother would order us to go get the chicken, which was impossible since the direction that the chicken took and the speed with which it ran were indeterminate. She didn't like us making our faces up in distaste at anything that had to do with eating or cleaning or washing. So, whoever let the chicken escape or whoever refused to go get it would have to stand holding it for five minutes until my grandmother made a few turns in the house, then they would have to pluck it and gut it and wrap the feathers and innards in newspaper, throwing it in the garbage. That person may well have to take the garbage out for a week. If you can eat, my grandmother would say, you can clean and you shouldn't scorn life.

One day we found a huge balloon down in the backyard. It was the biggest balloon we'd ever had and it wasn't even around Christmas time. Patsy Benjamin, who played through her fence with us, hidden by the rose mango tree from her Aunt Lena, forgot herself and started shouting that it was hers. She began crying and ran complaining to her aunt that we had stolen her balloon. Her aunt dragged her inside, and we ran around our house fighting and pulling at each other, swearing that the balloon belonged to this one or that one. My grandmother grabbed one of us on the fourth or fifth round and snatched the balloon away. We never understood the cause for this since it was such a find, and never quite understood my grandmother muttering something about Tante's son leaving his "nastiness" everywhere. Tante, herself, had been trying to get our attention as we raced round and round the house. This was our first brush with what was called "doing rudeness."

Later, when my big sister began to menstruate and stopped hanging around with us, we heard from our classmates that men menstruated too, and so we put two and two together and figured that Tante's son's nastiness must have to do with his menstruation.

On our way home from school one day, a rumour blazed its way through all the children just let out from school that there was a male sanitary napkin at the side of the road near the pharmacy on Royal Road. It was someone from the Catholic girl's school who started it, and troupe after troupe of school children hurried to the scene to see it. The rumour spread back and forth, along the Coffee, with school children corroborating and testifying that they had actually seen it. By the time we got there, we only saw an empty brown box which we skirted, a little frightened at first, then pressed in for a better view. There really wasn't very much more to see and we figured that someone must have removed it before we got there. Nevertheless, we swore that we had seen it and continued to spread the rumour along the way, until we got home, picking up the chant which was building as all the girls whipped their fingers at the boys on the street singing, "Boys have periods TOOOOOO!" We couldn't ask my grandmother if men had periods, but it was the source of weeks of arguing back and forth.

When my period came, it was my big sister who told me what to do. My grandmother was not there. By then, my mother had returned from England and an unease had fallen over us. Anyway, when I showed my big sister, she shoved a sanitary napkin and two pins at me and told me not to play with boys anymore and that I couldn't climb the mango tree any more and that I shouldn't fly around the yard anymore either. I swore everyone not to tell my mother when she got home from work, but they all did anyway and my mother with her air, which I could never determine since I never looked her in the face, said nothing.

My mother had returned. We had anticipated her arrival with a mixture of pride and fear. These added to an uncomfortable sense that things would not be the same, because in the weeks preceding her arrival my grandmother revved up the old warning about us not being able to be rude or disobey anymore, that we would have to be on our best behaviour to be deserving of this woman who had been to England, where children were not like us. She was my grandmother's favourite daughter too, so my grandmother was quite proud of her. When she arrived, some of us hung back behind my grandmother's skirt, embarrassing her before my mother who, my grandmother said, was expecting to meet well-brought up children who weren't afraid of people.

To tell the truth, we were expecting a white woman to come through the door, the way my grandmother had described my mother and the way the whole street that we lived on treated the news of my mother's return, as if we were about to ascend in their respect. The more my grandmother pushed us forward to say hello to my mother, the more we clung to her skirts, until she finally had to order us to say hello. In the succeeding months, my grandmother tried to push us toward my mother. She looked at us with reproach in her eyes that we did not acknowledge my mother's presence and her power. My mother brought us weiners and fried eggs and mashed potatoes, which we had never had before, and said that she longed for kippers, which we did not know. We enjoyed her strangeness but we were uncomfortable under her eyes. Her suitcase smelled strange and foreign, and for weeks despite our halting welcome of her, we showed off in the neighborhood that we had someone from away.

Then she began ordering us about and the wars began.

Those winters in England, when she must have bicycled to Hampstead General Hospital from which we once received a letter and a postcard with her smiling to us astride a bicycle, must have hardened the smile which my grandmother said that she had and which was dimly recognizable from the photograph. These winters, which she wrote about and which we envied as my sister read them to us, she must have hated. And the thought of four ungrateful children who deprived her of a new dress or stockings to travel London, made my mother unmerciful on her return.

We would run to my grandmother, hiding behind her skirt, or dive for the sanctuary of my grandmother's room. She would enter, accusing my grandmother of interfering in how she chose to discipline "her" children. We were shocked. Where my mother acquired this authority we could not imagine. At first my grandmother let her hit us, but finally she could not help but intervene and ask my mother if she thought that she was beating animals. Then my mother would reply that my grandmother had brought us up as animals. This insult would galvanize us all against my mother. A back answer would fly from the child in question who would, in turn, receive a slap from my grandmother, whereupon my grandmother would turn on my mother with the length of her tongue. When my grandmother gave someone the length of her tongue, it was given in a low, intense, and damning tone, punctuated by chest beating and the biblical, "I have nurtured a viper in my bosom."

My mother often became hysterical and left the house, crying what my grandmother said were crocodile tears. We had never seen an adult cry in a rage before. The sound in her throat was a gagging yet raging sound, which frightened us, but it was the sight of her tall, threatening figure which cowed us. Later, she lost hope that we would ever come around to her and she began to think and accuse my grandmother of setting her children against her. I recall her shoes mostly, white and thick, striding across the tiny house.

These accusations increased, and my grandmother began to talk of dying and leaving us. Once or twice, my mother tried to intervene on behalf of one or the other of us in a dispute with my grandmother. There would be silence from both my grandmother and us, as to the strangeness of this intervention. It would immediately bring us on side to my grandmother's point of view and my mother would find herself in the company of an old woman and some children who had a life of their own — who understood their plays, their dances, gestures, and signals, who were already intent on one another. My mother would find herself standing outside these gestures into which her inroads were abrupt and incautious. Each foray made our dances more secretive, our gestures subterranean.

Our life stopped when she entered the door of the house, conversations closed in mid-sentence, and elegant gestures with each other turned to sharp asexual movements.

My mother sensed these closures since, at first, we could not hide these scenes fast enough to escape her jealous glance. In the end, we closed our scenes ostentatiously in her presence. My grandmother's tongue lapping over a new story or embellishing an old one would become brusque in, "Tell your mother good evening." We, telling my grandmother a story or receiving her assurance that when we get rich, we would buy a this or a that, while picking out her gray hairs, would fall silent. We longed for when my mother stayed away. Most of all we longed for when she worked nights. Then we could sit all evening in the grand darkness of my grandmother's stories.

When the electricity went out and my grandmother sat in the rocking chair, the wicker seat bursting from the weight of her hips, the stories she spun, no matter how often we heard them, languished over the darkness whose thickness we felt, rolling in and out of the veranda. Some nights the darkness, billowing about us, would be suffused by the perfume of lady-of-the-night, a white, velvet, yellow, orchid-like flower which grew up the street in a neigh-bour's yard. My grandmother's voice, brown and melodic, about how my grandfather, "Yuh Papa, one dark night, was walking from Ortoire to Guayguayare. . . ."

The road was dark and my grandfather walked alone with his torchlight pointed toward his feet. He came to a spot in the road which suddenly chilled him. Then, a few yards later, he came to a hot spot in the road, which made him feel for a shower of rain. Then, up ahead, he saw a figure and behind him he heard its footsteps. He kept walking, the footsteps pursued him dragging a chain, its figure ahead of him. If he had stopped, the figure, which my grandfather knew to a *legahoo,* would take his soul; so my grandfather walked steadily, shining his torchlight at his feet and re-peating psalm twenty-three, until he passed the bridge by the sea wall and passed the savannah, until he arrived at St. Mary's, where he lived with my grandmother.

It was in the darkness on the veranda, in the honey chuckle back of my grandmother's throat, that we learned how to catch a *soucouyant* and a *lajabless* and not to an-swer to the "hoop! hoop! hoop!" of *duennes,* the souls of dead children who were not baptized, come to call liv-ing children to play with them. To catch a soucouyant, you had to either find the barrel of rain water where she had left her skin and throw pepper in it, or sprinkle salt or rice on your doorstep so that when she tried to enter the house to take your blood, she would have to count every grain of salt or rice before entering. If she dropped just one grain or miscounted, she would have to start all over again her impossible task, and in the mornings she would be discovered, distraught and without her skin, on the doorstep.

When we lived in the country before moving to the street, my grandmother had shown us, walking along the beach in back of the house, how to identify a duenne foot. She made it with her heel in the sand and then, without laying the ball of her foot down, imprinted her toes in the front of the heel print.

Back in the country, my grandmother walked outside and up and down the beach and cut coconut with a cutlass and dug chip-chip on the beach and slammed the kitchen window one night just as a mad man leapt to it to try to get into the house. My grandmother said that as a child in the country, my mother had fallen and hit her head, ever since which she had been pampered and given the best food to eat and so up to this day she was very moody and could go off her head at the slightest. My mother took this liberty whenever she returned home, skewing the order of our routines in my grandmother.

It seemed that my grandmother had raised more mad children than usual, for my uncle was also mad, and one time he held up a gas station which was only the second time that my grandmother had to leave the house, again on the arm of my big sister. We readied my grandmother then, and she and my big sister and I went to the courthouse on the Promenade to hear my uncle's case. They didn't allow children in, but they allowed my big sister as my grandmother had to lean on her. My uncle's case was not heard that morning, so we left the court and walked up to the Promenade. We had only gone a few steps when my grandmother felt faint. My sister held the smelling salts at her nostrils, as we slowly made our way as inconspicuously as we could to a bench near the bandstand. My grandmother cried, mopping her eyes with the handkerchief, and talked about the trouble her children had caused her. We, all three, sat on the bench on the Promenade near the bandstand, feeling stiff and uncomfortable. My grandmother said my uncle had allowed the public to wash their mouth in our family business. She was tired by then, and she prayed that my mother would return and take care of us so that she would be able to die in peace.

Soon after, someone must have written my mother to come home, for we received a letter saying that she was finally coming.

We had debated what to call my mother over and over again and came to no conclusions. Some of the words sounded insincere and disloyal, since they really belonged to my grandmother, although we never called her by those names. But when we tried them out for my mother, they hung so cold in the throat that we were discouraged immediately. Calling my mother by her given name was too presumptuous, even though we had always called all our aunts and uncles by theirs. Unable to come to a decision, we abandoned each other to individual choices. In the end, after our vain attempts to form some word, we never called my mother by any name. If we needed to address her, we stood about until she noticed that we were there and then we spoke. Finally, we never called my mother.

All of the words which we knew belonged to my grandmother. All of them, a voluptuous body of endearment, dependence, comfort, and infinite knowing. We were all full of my grandmother, she had left us full and empty of her. We dreamed in my grandmother and we woke up in her, bleary-eyed and gesturing for her arm, her elbows, her smell. We jockeyed with each other, lied to each other, quarrelled with each other and with her for the boon of lying close to her, sculpting ourselves around the roundness of her back. Braiding her hair and oiling her feet. We dreamed in my grandmother and we woke up in her, bleary-eyed and gesturing for her lap, her arms, her elbows, her smell, the fat flesh of her arms. We fought, tricked each other for the crook between her thighs and calves. We anticipated where she would sit and got there before her. We bought her achar and paradise plums.

My mother had walked the streets of London, as the legend went, with one dress on her back for years, in order to send those brown envelopes, the stamps from which I saved in an old album. But her years of estrangement had left her angry and us cold to her sacrifice. She settled into fits of fury. Rage which raised welts on our backs, faces, and thin legs. When my grandmother had turned away, laughing from us, saying there was no place to beat, my mother found room.

Our silences which once warded off hunger now warded off her blows. She took to mean impudence, and her rages whipped around our silences more furiously than before. I, the most ascetic of us all, sustained the most terrible moments of her rage. The more enraged she grew, the more silent I became, the harder she hit, the more wooden, I. I refined this silence into a jewel of the most sacred sandalwood, finely grained, perfumed, mournful yet stoic. I became the only inhabitant of a cloistered place carrying my jewel of fullness and emptiness, voluptuousness and scarcity. But she altered the silences profoundly.

Before, with my grandmother, the silences had company, were peopled by our hope. Now, they were desolate. She had left us full and empty of her. When someone took the time to check, there was no photograph of my grandmother, no figure of my grandmother in layers of clothing and odd-sided socks, no finger stroking the air in reprimand, no arm under her chin at the front window or crossed over her breasts waiting for us.

My grandmother had never been away from home for more than a couple of hours, and only three times that I could remember. So her absence was lonely. We visited her in the hospital every evening. They had put her in a room with eleven other people. The room was bare. You could see underneath all the beds from the doorway, and the floors were always scrubbed with that hospital-smelling antiseptic which reeked its own sickliness and which I detested for years after. My grandmother lay in one of the beds nearest the door, and I remember my big sister remarking to my grandmother that she should have a better room, but my grandmother hushed her saying that it was alright and anyway she wouldn't be there for long and the nurses were nice to her. From the chair beside my grandmother's bed in the hospital you could see the parking lot on Chancery Lane. I would sit with my grandmother, looking out the window and describing the scene to her. You could also see part of the wharf and the Gulf of Paria, which was murky where it held to the wharf. And St. Paul's church where I was confirmed, even though I did not know the catechism and only mumbled when Canon Fraquar drilled us in it.

Through our talks at the window my grandmother made me swear that I would behave for my mother. We planned, when I grew up and went away, that I would send for my grandmother and that I would grow up to be something good, that she and I and Eula and Ava and Kat and Genevieve would go to Guayaguayare and live there forever. I made her promise that she would not leave me with my mother.

It was a Sunday afternoon, the last time that I spoke with my grandmother. I was describing a bicycle rider in the parking lot and my grandmother promised to buy one for me when she got out of hospital.

My big sister cried and curled herself up beneath the radio when my grandmother died. Genevieve's face was wet with tears, her front braid pulled over her nose, she, sucking her thumb.

When they brought my grandmother home, it was after weeks in the white twelve-storey hospital. We took the curtains down, leaving all the windows and doors bare, in respect for the dead. The ornaments, doilies, and plastic flowers were removed, and the mirrors and furniture covered with white sheets. We stayed inside the house and did not go out to play. We kept the house clean and we fell into our routine of silence when faced with hunger. We felt alone. We did not believe. We thought that it was untrue. In disbelief, we said of my grandmother, "Mama can't be serious!"

The night of the wake, the house was full of strangers. My grandmother would never allow this. Strangers, sitting and talking everywhere, even in my grandmother's room. Someone, a great aunt, a sister of my grandmother, whom we had never seen before, turned to me sitting on the sewing machine and ordered me in a stern voice to get down. I left the room, slinking away, feeling abandoned by my grandmother to strangers.

I never cried in public for my grandmother. I locked myself in the bathroom or hid deep in the backyard and wept. I had learned, as my grandmother had taught me, never to show people your private business.

When they brought my grandmother home the next day, we all made a line to kiss her good-bye. My littlest sister was afraid; the others smiled for my grandmother. I kissed my grandmother's face hoping that it was warm.

Madame Alaird's Breasts

Madame Alaird was our French mistress. *"Bonjour, mes enfants,"* she would say on entering the classroom, then walk heavily toward her desk. Madame Alaird walked heavily because of her bosom which was massive above her thin waist. As she walked her breasts tipped her entire body forward. She was not tall, neither was she short, but her bosom made her look quite impressive and imposing and, when she entered our form room, her voice resonated through her breasts, deep and rich and Black, *"Bonjour, mes enfants."*

We, Form 3A, sing-songed back, "Bonjour, Ma-dame A-lai-air-d," smirking, as we watched her tipping heavily to her desk.

We loved Madame Alaird's breasts. All through the conjugation of verbs — *aller, acheter, appeller,* and *écouter* — we watched her breasts as she rested them on the top of her desk, the bodice of her dress holding them snugly, her deep breathing on the *eu* sounds making them descend into their warm cave and rise to take air. We imitated her voice but our *eu*'s sounded like shrill flutes, sharpened by the excitement of Madame Alaird's breasts.

We discussed Madame Alaird's breasts on the way home every Tuesday and Thursday, because French was every Tuesday and Thursday at 10:00 a.m. They weren't like Miss Henry's breasts. We would never notice Miss Henry's breasts anyway because we hated needlework and sewing. Miss Henry was our needlework and sewing mistress.

Madame Alaird wasn't fat. She wasn't thin either, but her breasts were huge and round and firm. Every Tuesday and Thursday, we looked forward to having Madame Alaird's breasts to gawk at, all of French period. Madame Alaird wore gold-rimmed bifocals which meant that she could not see very well, even though she peered over her bifocals pointedly in the direction of snickers or other rude noises during her teaching. But this was merely form; we doubted whether she could see us.

Madame Alaird's breasts were like pillows, deep purple ones, just like Madame Alaird's full lips as she expressed the personal pronouns,

"Je-u, Tu-ooo, Ell-lle, No-o-us. Mes enfants, encore. . . ."

"No-o-us, Vo-uus, Ell-lles," which we deliberately mispronounced to have Madame Alaird say them over. Madame Alaird's breasts gave us imagination beyond our years or possibilities, of burgundy velvet rooms with big-legged women and rum and calypso music. Next to Madame Alaird's breasts, we loved Madame Alaird's lips. They made water spring to our mouths just like when the skin bursts eating a purple fat mammy sipote fruit.

Every Tuesday and Thursday after school, bookbags and feet dragging, we'd discuss Madame Alaird's breasts.

"But you see Madame Alaird breasts!"

"Girl, you ever see how she just rest them on the table!"

"I wonder how they feel?"

"You think I go have breasts like Madame Alaird?"

Giggles.

"But Madame Alaird have more breasts than anybody I know."

"She must be does be tired carrying them, eh!"

Giggles, doubled over in laughter, near the pharmacy. Then past the boys' college,

"And you don't see how they sticking out in front like that and when she walk is like she falling over! Oui! Bon jieu!"

"But Madame Alaird ain't playing she have breast, oui!"

"And girl she know French, eh?"

"Madame Alaird must be could feed the whole world with them breasts, yes!"

Giggles reaching into belly laughs near Carib Street and in chorus,

"*BONJOUR, MES ENFANTS!*" rounding our lips on the *bonjour,* like Madame Alaird's kiss.

Madame Alaird was almost naked as far as we were concerned. It did not matter that she was always fully clothed. She was almost puritan in her style. Usually she wore brogues and ordinary clothing. Madame was not a snazzy dresser, but on speech day and other special occasions, she put on tan heels, stockings seamed up the back, a close-fitting beige dress with perhaps a little lace at the bosom, and her gold-rimmed bifocals hung from their gold string around her neck, resting on her breasts. Madame Alaird was beautiful. The bifocals didn't mean that Madame Alaird was old. She wasn't young either. She was what we called a full woman.

We heard that Madame Alaird had children. Heard, as adolescents hear, through self-composition. We got few glimpses of Madame Alaird's life, which is why we made up most of it. Once, we saw her husband come to pick her up after school. He drove an old sedate-looking dark green Hillman, and he was slim and short and quiet-looking with gold-rimmed peepers, like Madame Alaird's.

"But woii! Madame Alaird husband skinny, eh?!"

"It must be something when Madame Alaird sit down on him!"

That Tuesday or Thursday Madame Alaird's husband added fuel to the fire of Madame Alaird's breasts.

"He must be does have a nice time in Madame Alaird breast, oui."

"Madame Alaird must be feel sorry for him, that is why."

Madame Alaird went through a gloomy period where often the hem of her skirt hung and she wore a dark green dress with the collar frayed. We were very concerned because the period lasted a very long time and we knew that the other teachers and the head mistress were looking at her suspiciously. Among them, Madame Alaird stood out. They were not as pretty as she, though she wasn't *pretty,* for she was not a small woman, but she was as rosy as they were dry. In this time, she was absent-minded in class and didn't look at us, but looked at her desk and took us up sternly in our conjugations. Her breasts, hidden in dark green knit, were disappointing.

We were protective of Madame Alaird. In the wooden and musty paper smell of our thirteen-year-old girl lives, in the stifling, uniformed, Presbyterian hush of our days, in the bone and stick of our youngness, Madame Alaird was a vision, a promise of the dark-red fleshiness of real life.

"Madame Alaird looking like she catching trouble, eh?"

"But why she looking so bad?"

"It must be she husband, oui!"

"Madam Alaird don't need he."

"Is true! Madame Alaird could feed a country! How she could need he?"

"So he have Madame Alaird catching hell, or what?"

"Cheuupss! You don't see he could use a beating!"

"But Madame Alaird could beat he up easy, easy, you

know!"

"You ain't see how the head teacher watching she?"

"Hmmm!"

And so it went for months until, unaccountably, her mood changed. Unaccountably, because we were not privy to Madame Alaird's life and could see only glimpses, outward and filtered, of what might be happening in it. But our stories seemed to make sense. And we saw her breasts. The only real secret that we knew about her life. Anyway, Madame Alaird was back to herself and we lapped our tongues over her breasts once again, on Tuesdays and Thursdays.

"Girl! Alaird looking good again, eh."

"She must be send that old husband packing."

"She must be get a new 'thing'."

"You ain't see how she dress up nice, nice, woi!!"

We were jealous of Madame Alaird's husband and vexed with him for no reason at all. We even watched him cut-eyed when he came to pick her up from school.

"She must be find a new 'thing'! Oui foo!"

"Madame Alaird ain't playing she nice, non!"

So the talk about Madame Alaird's breasts went, for months and months, until we were so glad to see Madame Alaird's breasts again that we cooked up a treat to please her. The vogue that month was rubber spiders and snakes which we used to sneak up on each other and send down the boney backs of our still breastless bodices.

Our renewed obsession with Madame Alaird's breasts, our passion for their snug bounciness, their warm purpleness, their juicy fruitedness, had us giggling and whispering every time she walked down the hall and into Form 3A, our class. Madame Alaird's breasts drove us to extremes. She was delighted with our conjugations, rapturous about our attentiveness. Her *Bonjour, mes enfants* were more fleshy and sonorous, her *eu*'s and *ou*'s more voluptuous and dark-honeyed. We glowed at her and rivalled each other to be her favourite.

The plan was cooked up to place a rubber snake on Madame Alaird's chair, so that when she sat down she would jump up in fright. We had the idea that Madame Alaird would laugh at this trick and it would put us on even more familiar terms with her. So, that Tuesday, we put the plan in motion and stood in excited silence as Madame Alaird entered and tipped heavily toward her chair, a deeper, more sensuous than ever *Bonjour, mes enfants,* pushing out of her full, purple lips. All of us burst out, shaking with laughter as Madame Alaird sat, jumped up, uttered a muffled yell, all at the same time. Then standing, looking severely at us — we, doubled over in uncontroll- able laughter — she resounded, in English,

"When you are all ready to apologise, I shall be in the office. I shall not enter this class again until you do!" and strode out of the door.

After the apology, made in our our forty-voiced, flutey girls' chorus, after our class mistress ordered it, Madame Alaird returned and was distant. This did not stop our irreverence about Madame Alaird's breasts. We ignored the pangs of conscience (those of us who had any) about upsetting her and rolled out laughing, for days after. Lustful and unrepentant.

"You ain't see how Madame Alaird jump up!"

"Woi! Madame Alaird breasts just fly up in the air and bounce back down."

"Oui fooo! Bon Jieu! Was like she had wings."

"Madame Alaird ain't playing she have breasts, non!"

"Bon Jieu oiii!"

In her classes, we lowered our eyes to the burgundy velvet rooms of her beautiful breasts, like penitents.

No rinsed blue sky, no red flower fences

The apartment had tried to kill her again. She painted the walls as fast as she felt threatened. The city, she had been all through it in her searching, was dotted with bachelor apartments which she could not afford and hated anyway. As she moved from one to the other, she painted the walls. First yellow, to be bright, and then white, to be alone. She told her friends that it was so that she could fill the rooms with her own self, so that she could breathe and put up her own paintings, her own landscapes on the walls. She had to live there but she didn't have to lose all sense of beauty, with their tatty walls and nothing in them as if no one ever lived there. Out of embarrassment she never said, but it was also because somehow she thought that the creditors, the mornings full of bills, would go away or she could feel them gone in the blinding white. Even with the walls so clean she never had money and when she didn't have it most, the apartment scared her.

It was an old building, four stories (she hated high-rises), wooden floors and old stucco walls. It creaked every time someone passed in the corridors. When she had money the creaking sounded homely, like living with family. But when she was flat broke and depressed, the sound of footsteps outside the door made her jumpy. A queasy feeling appeared in her chest, as if a passage opened up between her throat and her heart and a fine and awful sound passed through, hurting the columns of arteries and the empty food cavity. The pain and the sound collapsed in her diaphragm. Her hand would reach to her soft stomach to assure the queasiness. But even her hands, as tender as they would have liked to have been, were frightened and upset the order of things, inciting her face and head to sadness and then reproach for such weakness and then pity for her blackness and her woman's body, and hopelessness at how foolish she was in not even being able to pay the rent, or fix her teeth, which she dreamt nightly fell out in her hands, bloodless.

Some mornings she woke up hearing the tree not far from her window sighing as an unexpected wind blew through it. Then she thought that she missed her children who were growing up far away without her. She wanted to gather up children and take them outside. They would like the sound, the island, the ferry. She could see their legs, bony and shine black, trembling to catch dirt and bruises.

The city could be so nasty when she had no money. Money was so important. If you had none, it made you feel as if you'd never done a thing in your life.

She'd worked "illegal" for six years. Taking care of children, holding their hands across busy streets, standing with them at corners which were incongruous to her colour, she herself incongruous to the little hands, held as if they were more precious than she, made of gold, and she just the black earth around. She was always uncomfortable under the passing gazes, muttering to herself that she knew, they didn't have to tell her that she was out of place here. But there was no other place to be right now. The little money fed her sometimes, fed her children back home, no matter the stark scene which she created on the corners of the street. She, black, silent and unsmiling; the child, white, tugging and laughing, or whining.

The city was claustrophobic. She felt land-locked. Particularly on humid days in the summer. She wanted to rush to the beach. But not the lake. It lay stagnant and saltless at the bottom of the city. She needed a piece of water which led out, the vast ocean, salty and burning on the eyes. The feel of the salt, blue and moving water, rushing past her ears and jostling her body, cleaning it, coming up a different person each time as she dove through a curling wave. Not knowing how it would turn out. A feeling of touching something quite big. She always imagined and tasted that plunge into the sea, that collision with the ocean. Suddenly every two years she felt like leaving, going to dive into the ocean just once. Scratch the money up, beg for it, borrow, work back-breaking weeks scrubbing floors — but leave.

Some mornings she woke up looking up through the blind, the building, cloud, sky, surface. If the rain had fallen, rinsed blue, she hoped that the sea would be outside the apartment. Just there, just a few steps away. Some mornings she'd hear a small plane in the sky, a plane that would only fly over water, grass, and red-wrung flower fences. The sea must be outside if all the sounds, plane tree, eleven o'clock and rinsed blue sky were there. She lay on the floor loving the sound, making ready to see the sea a few steps from her window.

The threat of being evicted hung over her head. She thought that when she walked in the street, people noticed. They must've. If there was anything that tipped them off, it was the sign she wore in her eyes. She kept them lowered, or at courageous times she stared until they removed their own eyes. On the bus, when she had the fare, she always stood, trying to appear thinner than she was, bent, staring out the window. She did not ask for apologies when people jostled her; she pretended that it did not happen. She did try sometimes. Sitting in two seats and ignoring people coming in, but by the time two or three stops had passed she would ring the bell, get off the bus, and walk quickly home.

Returning home her imagination tightened the walls of the apartment giving them a cavernous, gloomy look. She would lie on the floor and listen for footsteps in the corridor outside. The phone would ring and startle her. The sound would blast around in her chest and she would pray for it to stop, never thinking to answer it. It would course its way through her arms so that when she looked at her fingers they would seem odd, not hers or she, not theirs. Frightened until it stopped, then anxious at perhaps having missed a friend listening to the ringing on the other side. Some of her friends knew that she never answered the phone and so would let it ring; but even though she knew the signal, she worried that perhaps other people, other than friends, had caught on. So when the ringing continued she was more afraid, thinking how persistent her enemies were.

The apartment had two rooms. She needed a place with two rooms. Each so that she could leave the other. The large room, when it was painted and when she threw out the bed, seemed like someone else's place.

After she had sent the baby home, she had thrown the

bed out. It was only a reminder of the long nine months and the hospital staff's cold eyes. When she'd left with the new baby she had pretended that someone was coming for her, waiting for her outside. But no one was there, no one knew, and the name she had used was not hers. Nor did the baby exist. No papers. She would be found out if she registered the little girl. So small and wiry and no papers.

In the smaller room she kept a desk with a light to one corner. Two short black shelves were stuffed with books and papers which she could not throw out because she might need them as evidence that she tried to pay this bill or that one. She wrote anonymous letters to the immigration department asking if maybe she gave up would they still send her home . . . would they please have pity for her children.

A peacock rattan chair sat under the poster of home. A girl in a wet T-shirt, the sea in back, the sun on her body, represented home. Home had never been like that, but she kept the poster. Its glamour shielded her from the cold outside and the dry hills back home at the same time. The chair creaked everytime the humidity in the room changed.

In the days after she had read *Siddhartha*, someone had given it to her saying she would find peace, she lay for hours chanting *om*. She attributed the creaking chair to the spirit of her great grandmother coming to visit. And for at least two months chanting *om* helped to calm her now chronic worrying. She sat cross-legged, her back vertical to the floor of her room, her hands, thumb, and index finger softly clasped. So she buried the sound of the footsteps outside her door in a long breathy *om,* hoping that this one syllable expressed the universe. She actually saw the deep-blue softing shape of *om,* approached its glowing dark, telling herself that this would save her from the thin, sharp voices on the phone, the girl in the wet

T-shirt, the child with the white hand, the lewd traffic whirling in the middle of the street.

Once when she was nine, a long time ago, she'd seen a woman, old, bathing herself on the edge of the sand and water, dipping a cup, lifting it to her head, rubbing the shade of her long flacid breasts. How bold, she thought, then walked past and turned slightly to see her again, still there, her face sucked to her bones, her eyes watery from age, unblinking. The woman, the gesture had stayed with her, marked her own breasts, her eyes. She willed herself not to feel hungry but to stay alive, present. She would lessen the number of her movements, she would design efficient strokes, nothing wasted. She would become the old woman. But how could she, so far from there.

There was a fireplace in the large room. Not a real one. One of those with two electric ranges strung across. It should have been real for its ornate facade. It may have been copper underneath the crude layers of paint. After two years of living in the apartment, she discovered that the fireplace worked. She found this out through the woman across the hall who invited her to a christmas party. The woman was Jamaican, she had a fifteen-year-old daughter coming to meet her soon, and a man friend who came every two weeks to sleep in the daytime on Sundays. He was tall, round, with a prickly thick moustache. The woman, short, round, pulled her hair tightly back on these occasions. The rest of the time she wore it wild. All this she learnt by looking through the peephole at ther neighbour when she was not afraid to look in the hallway.

Still, of all the places she had lived, she felt the strongest here. After years of dodging the authorities and the bill collectors, she had acquired some skill in putting them off. She realized that rudeness and sometimes a frank, "I don't have any money," would do. She consoled herself that there was no debtors prison and often, when she could bring up the nerve, told them, "Take me to court." But creditors had more stamina than she and they would keep calling and threatening and she would break down and promise them her life. One had told her to go and sell her body if she had to and why were you people coming to this country, if you couldn't pay your bills, he had yelled into her ear. Her days then were heady. Each ring of the phone, each footstep in the hall, each knock on the door threatened to blow everything to hell. Those days the white walls came alive, glaring at her, watching her as she slept fitfully.

Mostly she did not remember her dreams. And mostly they were full of her watching herself as a guest at some occasion. She played all the parts in her dreams. Dreamer, dreamed. She was female and male, neutral. She never dreamed of anything that she was not. When she practiced to fly in her dreams, it was she who flew. Swooping down like a pelican into the water and changing course upward before touching. She had rehearsed that swooping since she was three, noticing the pelican's clumsy transforming glide into the sea at Point Fortin by the sea, its wet, full exit, its throat expanding fishlike. And she had practiced never reaching things too. One day a grove of orange balisier growing not far from the house caught her eye. After what seemed like hours of walking she never arrived at the grove and cried loudly until someone came to get her sitting in the dirt road.

Dreamer remained the same and often less than dreamed. It would surprise her to awaken to her thin, unvoluptuous body, limited to the corner of the floor on which she slept. Dreamed would return to limitlessness and the dreamer, to the acute clarity of the real — the orange juice, the telephone, the white Toronto street in winter.

Her sleeping was worse in the winter. There was an urgency to sleep at any hour. Especially when she had not seen the sun for days. A kind of pressure brought on by the gray sky, which she opened her eyes to on winter mornings, packed itself around her temples. It made her eyelids feel swollen and she spent half the day trying to recover herself. Each morning she would have to convince herself to get up from her half sleep which would made her sick. This half-sleep did not belong to the dreamer or the dreamed. The avoided telephone calls recurred, answer no, ring no, answer, cupped to her mouth; the empty stomach; looking for a job, four hundred University eighth, no tenth floor, the immigration department, the smell of the lobby, it rose from the carpet, mixed with the air conditioner and the thud of the elevators. People hunched their shoulders, all the women, she included, perfumed to sickness, nylon encasing their legs, stood stiffly in the elevator . . . pleading with someone there . . . would they send her home, would they pity her children please. . . .

She fled. She could only perfect this flight in her dream. Rushing outside to the street, she plunged into the sea of snow, wrapped bodies, snorting cars making clouds of smoked ice. Reaching the subway, she rode to the end, where the work crowd thinned out — High Park, Runnymede, Old Mill. Coming up, the train reached a bare sky, scarred trees, gully, apartment building, stopping. She came out, let the train pass, sat looking through the glass of the station. She sat there for hours, getting back on the train, changing stations, only to find herself sometimes back in the elevator trying not to breath the perfume, the smell of whiteness around her, a dull choking smell.

Wrestling to wake up, she tried to pull herself out of this half-sleep which belonged to things out of her control.

Movements rushed against each other. Shorter distances, more brusque, inhabited this sleep. Jumping to her feet, she realized that she was asleep. For the act of jumping found her lying, still on the floor, now surrounded by her body and her heavy face, with a film of flesh and thought to remove before rising and trying to decide what to do next.

The room becoming clearer than its uncharted corners. The tree over the next apartment building in the shadow of her thoughts, spread out its meagre twigs to form a shield against the cold, heavy air. Rushing to the window she looked at the street below, empty of people, still dark.

. . . this day if the sky could not move, if the heavy angle of the air would not shift to some other colour, at the corner she would knead a headache from her brow, walk to the middle of the street, the glowing centre of the wide lewd road and kneel down. . . .

Rushing to the window she looked at the street below, empty of people, still dark. Not sea and blue, no red flower fence and high sky.

Midday found her on the street corner, a little white hand in hers, her other hand kneading a headache from her brow.

At the Lisbon Plate

The sky in the autumn is full of telephone and telegraph wires; it is not like sitting in the Portuguese bar on Kensington in the summer, outside — the beer smell, the forgetful waiter. I wonder what happened to Rosa. She was about forty and wore a tight black dress, her face appliquéd with something I could barely identify as life. Her false mole, the one she wore beside her mouth, shifted every day and faded by evening. She had a look that was familiar to me. Possibly she had lived in Angola or Mozambique and was accustomed to Black women, so she looked at me kindly, colonially.

"Do you have fish, Rosa?" I would ask.

"Oh yes, good Portuguese fish."

"From the lake or from the sea."

"Ah the sea, of course."

This would be our conversation every time I would come to the bar, her "of course" informing me of her status in our relationship.

My life was on the upswing, and whenever that happened I went to the bar on Kensington. That was usually in

95

the summertime. After twenty years and half my life in this city I still have to wait for the summertime to get into a good mood. My body refuses to appreciate dull, gray days. Truthfully, let me not fool you, my life was neither up nor down, which for me is an upswing, and I don't take chances, I celebrate what little there is. Which is why I come to this bar. This is my refuge, as it is. I believe in contradictions.

So Rosa ran from Angola and Mozambique. Well, well! By the looks of it she'd come down a peg or two. At the Lisbon Plate, Rosa seems quite ordinary, quite different from the woman who entertained in the European drawing rooms in Luanda and Lorenças Marques. Then, she gave orders to Black women, whom she called *as pretinhas.* Then, she minced over to the little consul from Lisbon and the general, whose family was from Oporto and whom she made promise to give her a little gun for her protection when the touble started.

I figured anyone who left Angola was on the other side, on the run. Rosa did have a kind enough look, personally. The wholesale merchant she was married to or his general manager, whom she slept with from time to time, had to leave. So, Rosa left too. This does not absolve Rosa however. I'm sure that she acquired her plumpness like a bed bug, sucking a little blood here, a little there.

As I've said, my life was on the upswing. Most other times it was a bitch. But I had spent two successive days with no major setbacks. Nobody called me about money, nobody hurt my feelings, and I didn't wake up feeling shaky in the stomach about how this world was going. And, I had twenty clear bucks to come to the bar. This is my refuge. It is where I can be invisible or, if not invisible, at least drunk. Drinking makes me introspective, if not suicidal. In these moments I have often looked at myself from the third floor window of the furniture store across from the bar. Rheumy-eyed, I have seen a woman sitting there, whom I recognize as myself. A Black woman, legs apart, chin resting in the palm of her hand, amusement and revulsion travelling across her face in uneasy companionship. The years have taken a bit of the tightness out of my skin but the expression has not changed, searching and uneasy, haunted like a plantation house. Surrounded by the likes of Rosa and her compadres. A woman in enemy territory.

It has struck me more than once that a little more than a century ago I may have been Rosa's slave and not more that twenty-five years ago, her maid, whom she maimed, playing with the little gun that she got from the general from Aporto. My present existence is mere chance, luck, syzygy.

Rosa's brother, Joao the priest, was now living in New Jersey. He used to live in Toronto, but before that he lived in Angola. One day, in a village there, during the liberation war, two whites were kidnapped and the others, including Rosa's brother, the priest, went into the village and gunned down a lot of people — women, children, to death, everything. He told this story to Maria de Conseçao, my friend, and she told me. Women and children, everything. People think that saying women and children were killed makes the crime more disgusting. I was sorry that Maria de Conseçao told me, because whenever I think about it I see Joao the priest confiding this crime as if he relished it, rather than repented it. I think Maria de Conseçao told me the story just to get rid of it. It's the kind of story which occurs to you when you're doing something pleasant and it's the kind of story you can't get rid of. I've kept it.

I am not a cynical woman under ordinary circumstances, but if you sit here long enough, anyone can see how what appears to be ordinary, isn't.

For, on the other hand, I look like a woman I met many years ago. As old as dirt, she sat at a roadside waiting her time, an ivory pipe stuck in her withered lips and naked as she was born. That woman had stories, more lucid than mine and more frightening for that.

The day I met her, her bones were black powder and her fingers crept along my arm causing me to shiver. She was a dangerous woman. I knew it the moment I saw her and I should have left her sitting there, the old gravedigger. But no. Me, I had to go and look. I had to follow that sack of dust into places I had no right being. Me, I had to look where she pointed. She wanted to show me her condiments and her books. I thought nothing of it. Why not humour an old woman, I said in my mind. They were old as ashes. All tied up and knotted in a piece of cloth and, when she opened it up, you would not believe the rattling and the odour, all musty and sweet. A bone here and a fingernail there. They looked like they'd been sitting in mud for centuries, like her. When it came to the books, it was before they had pages and the writing was with stones, which the old thing threw on the ground and read to me. I never laughed so much as I laughed at her jokes, not to mention her stories which made me cry so much I swore I'd turn to salt water myself. It was one of her stories which led me here, in search of something I will recognize, once I see it.

But back to things that we can understand, because I want to forget that harridan in the road and her unpleasantness.

Today I am waiting for Elaine, as usual. She likes to make entrances of the type that white girls make in movies. The truth is she's always getting away from something or someone. She is always promising too much and escaping. Which is why we get along. I never believe a promise and I, myself, am in constant flight.

Elaine is a mysterious one. Two days ago she told me to meet her here at one o'clock. I've been sitting here ever since. I know that she'll turn up a new woman. She'll say that she's moving to Tanzania to find her roots. She'll have her head tied in a wrap and she'll have gold bracelets running up her arms. She'll be learning Swahili, she'll show me new words like *jambo* and she'll be annoyed if I don't agree to go with her. Elaine wants to be a queen in ancient Mali or Songhai. A rich woman with gold and land.

The bar has a limited view of Kensington market. Across the street from it there's a parkette, in the centre of which there is a statue of Cristobal Colon. Columbus, the carpetbagger. It's most appropriate that they should put his stoney arse right where I can see it. I know bitterness doesn't become me, but that son of a bitch will get his soon enough too. The smell from the market doesn't bother me. I've been here before, me and the old lady. We know the price of things. Which is why I feel safe in telling stories here. They will be sure to find me. For fish you must have bait; for some people you must have blood. Spread the truth around enough, and you must dig up a few liars.

In the summertime, I come to the bar practically every day. After my first beer I'm willing to talk to anyone. I'm willing to reveal myself entirely. Which is a dirty habit, since it has made me quite a few enemies. Try not to acquire it. The knots in my head loosen up and I may start telling stories about my family.

I keep getting mixed up with old ladies. For instance, I have an old aunt, she used to be beautiful. Not in the real sense, but in that sense that you had to be, some years ago.

Hair slicked back to bring out the Spanish and hide the African. You could not resemble your mother or your father. This would only prove your guilt. This aunt went mad in later years. I think that it must have been from so much self-denial or, given the way that it turned out. . . .

Anyway, when I was a child we used to go to their house. It was made of stone and there was a garden around it. A thick green-black garden. A forest. My aunt worked in the garden every day, pruning and digging. There was deep red hibiscus to the far right wall. The soil was black and loose and damp and piled around the roots of roses and xoras and anthuriums and orchids. In the daylight, the garden was black and bright; in the night, it was shadowy and dark. Only my aunt was allowed to step into the garden. At the edges, shading the forest-garden, were great calabash mango trees. Their massive trunks and roots gave refuge from my aunt when she climbed into a rage after merely looking at us all day. She would run after us screaming, "Beasts! Worthless beasts!" Her rage having not subsided, she would grab us and scrub us, as if to take the black out of our skins. Her results would never please her. Out we would come five still bright-black little girls, blackness intent on our skins. She would punish us by having us stand utterly still, dressed in stiffly starched dresses.

Elaine never reveals herself and she is the most frustrating storyteller. She handles a story as if stories were scarce. "Well," she says, as she sits down at the table. Then she pauses, far too long a pause, through which I say, in my mind, "I'm going to last out this pause." Then quickly getting upset, I say, "For god's sake, tell me." Then I have to drag it out of her, in the middle of which I say, "Forget it, I don't want to hear," then she drops what she thinks is the sinker and I nonchalantly say, "Is that it?" to which she swears that never again would she tell me a story. The truth is that Elaine picks up on great stories, but the way she tells them makes people suffer. I, on the other hand, am quite plain. Particularly when I'm in my waters. Drink, I mean. I've noticed that I'm prepared to risk anything. But truthfully, what makes a good story if not for the indiscretions we reveal, the admissions of being human. In this way, I will tell you some of my life; though I must admit that some of it is fiction, not much mind you, but what is lie, I do not live through with any less tragedy. Anyway, these are not state secrets, people live the way that they have to and handle what they can. But don't expect any of the old woman's tales. There are things that you know and things that you tell. Well, soon and very soon, as they say.

Listen, I can drink half a bottle of whisky and refuse to fall down. It's from looking at Rosa that I get drunk and it's from looking at Rosa that I refuse to fall down. I was a woman with a face like a baby before I met Rosa, a face waiting to hold impressions.

I saw the little minx toddle over to the statue of Columbus, the piss-face in the parkette, and kiss his feet. Everyone has their rituals, I see. And then, before her mirror, deciding which side to put the mole on. Her face as dry as a powder. Perfuming herself in her bedroom in Lorençes Marques, licking the oil off that greasy merchant of hers. Even though the weather must have been bad for her, she stuck it out until they were driven away. It's that face that Rosa used cursing those "sons of bitches in the bush," when the trouble started. "When the trouble started," indeed. These European sons of bitches always say "when the trouble started" when *their* life in the colonies begins to get miserable.

I never think of murder. I find it too intimate and there's a smell in the autumn that I do not like. I can always tell.

The first breath of the fall. It distracts me from everyone. I will turn down the most lucrative dinner invitation to go around like a bloodhound smelling the fall. Making sure and making excuses, suggesting and insinuating that the summer is not over. But of course, as soon as I get a whiff of that smell I know. It's the autumn. Then the winter comes in, as green and fresh as spring and I know that I have to wait another ten months for the old woman's prophecy to come true. That hag by the road doesn't know what she gave me and what an effort I must make to see it through. On top of that, I have to carry around her juju belt full of perfidious mixtures and insolent smells and her secrets. Her secrets. My god, you don't know what a soft pain in the chest they give me. I grow as withered as the old hag with their moaning. She's ground them up like seasoning and she's told me to wear them close to my skin, like a poultice. I thought nothing of it at first. A little perfume, I said, a little luxury. I now notice that I cannot take the juju off. I life up my camisole and have a look. It's hardly me there anymore. There's a hole like a cave with an echo.

The old hag hates the winter too; says it dries her skin out. God knows she's no more than dust, but vain as hell. She migrates like a *soucouyant* in the winter, goes back to the tropics, says she must mine the Sargasso for bones and suicides. I must say, I envy the old bagsnatcher. Though she's promised me her memories, her maps, and her flight plans when it's over. Until then, I wait and keep watch here, frozen like a lizard in Blue Mountain, while she suns her quaily self in some old slave port.

At this bar, as I have my first beer and wait for the African princess, Elaine, I discover substantive philosophical arguments concerning murder. The beauty is, I have a lot of time. I have watched myself here, waiting. A woman so old her skin turned to water, her eyes blazing like a dead candle. I'm starting to resemble that bag of dust, the longer I live.

Now they have a man waiting on tables at the bar. I suppose the pay must be better. Elaine says he resembles Rosa except for her beauty mole and her breasts. It doesn't matter how Rosa looks in her disguises, I am doomed to follow her like a bloodhound after a thief. He is quite forgetful. Twenty minutes ago I asked him for another beer and up to now he hasn't brought it. Elaine's the one who got me into beer drinking anyway. In the old days — before the great mother old soul in the road and before I sussed out Rosa and her paramour, Elaine and I used to roam the streets together, looking. The old bone digger must have spotted my vacant look then. Elaine, on the other hand, had very definite ideas. Even then Elaine was looking for a rich African to help her make her triumphal return to the motherland.

Still, a rumour went around that Elaine and I were lovers. It wouldn't have bothered either of us if it were true at the time or if it wasn't said in such a malicious way. But it was because of how we acted. Simply, we didn't defer to the men around and we didn't sleep with them, or else when we did we weren't their slaves forever or even for a while. So both factions, those we slept with and those we didn't, started the rumour that we were lovers. Actually, Elaine and I laughed at the rumours. We liked to think of ourselves as free spirits and realists. We never attempted to dispel the rumours; it would have taken far too much of a commitment to do that. It would be a full-time job of subjecting yourself to any prick on two legs. And anyway, if the nastiest thing that they could say about you is that you loved another woman, well. . . .

Elaine and I would take the last bus home, bags full of

unopened beer, or pay a taxi, after I had persuaded her that the man she was looking at was too disgusting to sleep with, just for a ride home. Elaine takes the practical to the absurd sometimes.

We've been to other bars. Elaine looked for the bars, she scouted all the hangouts. She determined the ambience, the crowd, and then she asked me to meet her there. There's no accounting for her taste. I'd get to the appointed bar and it would be the grungiest, with the most oily food, the most vulgar, horrible men and a juke box with music selected especially to insult women. This was during Elaine's nationalist phase. Everything was culture, rootsy. The truth is, I only followed Elaine to see if I could shake the old woman's stories or, alternately, if I could find the something for her and get her off my back. It's not that I don't like the old schemer. At first I didn't mind her, but then she started to invade me like a spirit. So I started to drink. You get drunk enough and you think you can forget, but you get even greater visions. At the beginning of any evening the old woman's stories are a blip on the horizon; thirteen ounces into a bottle of scotch or four pints of beer later the stories are as lurid as a butcher's block.

I had the fever for two days and dreamt that the stove had caught afire. My big sister was just standing there as I tried furiously to douse the fire which kept getting bigger and bigger. Finally, my sister dragged the stove from the wall and with a knowledgeable air, put the fire out. When I woke up, I heard that the stock exchange in Santiago had been blown up by a bomb in a suitcase and that some group called the communist fighting cell had declared war on NATO by destroying troop supply lines in Belgium. Just as I was thinking of Patrice Lumumba. For you, Patrice! From this I surmised that my dreams have effects. Though, they seem somewhat unruly. They escape me. They have fires in them and they destine at an unknown and precipitous pace.

I followed Elaine through her phases, though there were some that she hid from me. Now we come to this bar, where we cannot understand the language most of the time. Here Elaine plans the possibilities of living grandly and, if not, famously. As for me, I tolerate her dreams because when Elaine found this bar I knew it was my greatest opportunity. All of the signs were there. The expatriates from the colonial wars, the moneychangers and the skin dealers, the whip handlers, the coffle makers and the boatswains. Their faces leathery from the African sun and the tropical winter. They were swilling beer like day had no end. Rosa was in her glory, being pawed and pinched. Of course, they didn't notice me in my new shape. Heavens, I didn't notice me. It scared the hell out of me when the juju surged to my head and I was a thin smoke over the Lisbon Plate. What a night! They said things that shocked even me, things worse than Joao, the priest. The old-timers boasted about how many *piezas de indias* they could pack into a ship for a bauble or a gun. The young soldiers talked about the joys of filling a Black with bullets and stuffing a Black cunt with dynamite. Then they gathered around Columbus, the whoremaster, and sang a few old songs. The old woman and I watched the night's revelry with sadness, the caves in our chest rattling the echo of unkindness, but I noticed the old woman smiling as she counted them, pointing and circling with her hand, over and over again, mumbling, "Jingay, jingay where you dey, where you dey, where you dey, spirit nah go away." Before you know it, I was mumbling along with her too, "Jingay, jingay, where you dey. . . ." We stayed with them all night, counting and mumbling. Now, all I have to do is choose the day and the spot and it's done. The old woman loves fanfare and flourish, so it will have to be spectacular. If Elaine knew what a find this bar was, she'd charge me money.

Elaine never cared for Rosa one way or the other, which is where Elaine and I are different. Some people would have no effect on her whatsoever. This way she remained friends with everyone. Me, I hate you or I love you. Always getting into fights, always adding enemies to my lists. Which is why I'll never get any place, as they say. But Elaine will. Elaine, sadly, is a drunk without vision. I, unfortunately, am a drunk with ideas. Which is probably why the old woman chose me to be her steed.

I pride myself with keeping my ear to the ground. I read the news and I listen to the radio every day, even if it is the same news. I look for nuances, changes in the patter. It came to me the other night, when listening to the news. One Polish priest had been killed and the press was going wild. At the same time, I don't know how many African labourers got killed and, besides that, fell to their deaths from third-floor police detention rooms in Johannesburg; and all that the scribes talked about was how moderate the Broderbond is. We should be grateful I supppose.

It occurred to me that death, its frequency, causes, sequence and application to written history, favours, even anticipates, certain latitudes. The number of mourners, their enthusiasms, their entertainments, their widows' weeds, all mapped by a cartographer well schooled in pre-Galileo geography. I'm waxing. Don't stop me. I couldn't tell you the things I know.

Meanwhile back at the bar, still waiting for Elaine to surface, there have been several interesting developments. Speaking of politics. First, I hear that the entire bourgeoisie of Bolivia is dead. It was on the radio not more than half an hour ago. The deaths are not significant in and of themselves. What is interesting is that only a few days ago, when I heard that president Suazo was kidnapped in La Paz and that there was possibly a coup, I said in my mind that the entire bourgeoisie should perish. It was the Bolivian army who killed Ernesto Che Guevara, you see. They put his body in the newspapers with their smiles. Now, I hear the news that the entire bourgeoisie of Bolivia is dead. Of course, from this I learned that as I become more and more of a spirit, I have more and more possibilities. First Santiago and Belgium and now Bolivia.

Second, and most, most important, the big white boy has arrived here. He's ordered a beer from Rosa's brother. I would know those eyes anywhere. The last time I saw them, I was lying in the hold of a great ship leaving Conakry for the new world. It was just a glimpse, but I remember as if it were yesterday. I am a woman with a lot of time and I have waited, like shrimp wait for tide. I have waited, like dirt waits for worms. That hell-hole stank of my own flesh before I left it, its walls mottled with my spittle and waste. For days I lived with my body rotting and the glare of those eyes keeping me alive, as I begged to die and follow my carcass. This is the story the old road woman told me. Days and days and night and nights, dreaming death like a loved one; but those hellish eyes kept me alive and dreadfully human until reaching a port in the new world. His pitiless hands placed me on a block of wood like a yoke, when my carcass could not stand any more, for the worms had eaten my soul. Running, running a long journey over hot bush, I found a cliff one day at the top of an island and jumped — jumped into the jagged blue water of an ocean, swimming, swimming to Conakry.

Elaine has also arrived and disappeared again, she's always disappearing into the bar to make phone calls. I never get an explanation of these phone calls mainly because I simply continue with my story. But I have the feeling, as the afternoon progresses into evening, and as different moods cross Elaine's face after every phone call, that some crisis is being made, fought, and resolved. I have a feeling that Elaine needs my stories as a curtain for her equally spyish dramas.

The big white boy was sitting with his dog. I did not see his face at first, but I recognized him as you would recognize your hands. His hair was cut with one patch down the middle. He was wearing black and moaning as he sat there smoking weed. Like Rosa, he had fallen on his luck. I heard him say this.

"I don't have nobody, no friends, I ain't got no love, no nothing, just my dog."

He was blond. At least, that was the colour of his hair presently. I felt for him the compassion of a warship, the maudlin sentiment of a boot stepping on a face. He said this to Rosa, who gave him an unsympathetic look as she picked her teeth. I'm not fooled by their lack of affection for each other. They are like an alligator and a parasite. I felt like rushing to his throat, but something held me back. The old woman's burning hand. I've seen him and Rosa whispering behind my back. What would a punk ku klux klansman and a washed-up ex-colonial siren have in common. Except me and the old lady. I suppose they're wondering who I am. Wonder away you carrion! I wonder if they recognize me as quickly as I, them. I saw them do their ablutions on the foot of the statue in the parkette. How lovingly they fondled his bloody hands. They have their rituals, but I've lived longer than they.

Listen, I neglected to say that my old aunt of the forest has gone mad. She told my sister, and indeed the whole town of Monas Bay, that on Easter Sunday of 1979, this year, jesus christ had descended from the heavens and entered her bedroom and had been there ever since. She had had a vision. After days of fasting and kneeling on the mourning ground, she had entered a desert where nothing grew. No water and inedible shrubs. The sun's heat gave the air a glassiness upon looking into the distance. Then she saw christ. He was withered and young as a boy of twenty. Christ and my aunt conversed for many days and planned to marry three years from the time of their meeting. They would have a son who would grow to be the new christ. My aunt related this incident to any one who would listen and cursed into hell and damnation anyone who did not believe. Few, needless to say, didn't. Anyone with a vision was helpful in bad times and people said that at least she had the guts to have a vision, which was not like the politicians in those parts.

Even my aunt's garden had descended into sand and tough shrub. It had become like the desert of her vision. She no longer made any attempt to grow plants, she said that armageddon was at hand anyway. Her bedroom, she turned into a shrine on the very day of her meeting with christ. On the wall hung bits of cardboard with glossy photographs of her fiancé cut out of the *Plain Truth*, and candles burnt endlessly in the four corners of the shrine. Sundry chaplets of jumbie beads, plastic and ivory manoeuvred themselves on the windows and bedposts. My aunt knows that some people think that she is mad; so, in the style of her affianced, she prays for their salvation. If she is mad. . .which is a debate that I will never personally enter, having seen far too much in my short life and knowing that if you live in places with temporary electricity and plenty of hard work, jesus christ (if not god) is extant. Not to mention that, the last time that I saw her, she stood at what was once the gate to the forest garden and was now dead wire, wearing a washed-out flowered dress and her last remaining tooth, even though she was only a woman of fifty, and told me that the land taxes for the forest and the stone house were paid up or would be as soon as she went to town. This, to me, attested to her sanity. Come hell or high water, as they say, though these might be the obvious causes of her madness, if she were mad, they were certainly legal. Anyway, if she is mad, her vision is clearly not the cause of it. Rather it has made her quite sane. At any rate she no longer uses face powder.

This trick that I learned in Bolivia and the dream in Santiago has set me to thinking. She, the old poui stick, is not the only one who can have plans. The dear old lady only gave me seven red hot peppers and told me to write their names seven times on seven scraps of paper. Then put the seven pieces of paper into the seven red hot peppers and throw them into seven latrines. This, she said, would do for them. This and sprinkling guinea pepper in front of their door every morning. Then, she said, I should wait for the rest. The old hag is smart, but she never anticipated the times or perhaps that's what she means.

Elaine thinks I'm taking things too far, of course. But, I cannot stand this endless waiting. I've practically turned into a spirit with all this dreadfulness around the Lisbon Plate. I want to get back to my life and forget this old woman and her glamourous ideas. So, what must be done, must be done. Elaine's on her way to Zaire, at any moment anyway. I think she's landed Mobutu Sese Seku.

For now I've taken to hiding things from her. She doesn't care about anything. Each time I mention it she says, "Oh for god's sake, forget them." As if it's that easy. You tell me! When there's a quaily skinned battle-axe riding on your shoulder and whispering in your ear. Well fine, if Elaine can have her secret telephone calls, and I don't think that I mentioned her disappearances, I can have my secret fires too. She can't say that I didn't try to warn her.

Wait! Well, I'll be damned! They're coming in like flies, old one. I eavesdrop on conversations here. I listen for plots, hints. You never know what these people are up for. This way, I amuse myself and scout for my opportunity. Listen,

"Camus' *Outsider* can be interpreted as the ultimate alienation!"

Ha! Did you hear that? Now, literature! Jesus. That's the one who looks like a professor, all scruffy and sensitive. If the truth be known several hundred years ago he made up the phrase "Dark Ages," then he attached himself to an expedition around the Bight of Benin from which, as the cruder of his sea company packed human cargo into the hold of their ship, he rifled the gold statues and masks and he then created a "museum of primitive art" to store them. Since his true love was phrase-making, he made up "museum of primitive art," elaborating his former success "Dark Ages." Never trust white men who look sensitive. They're the worst kind of phonies. They want the best of both worlds. Compared to him, the big white boy looks like a saint.

Anyway, alienation, my ass! Camus! Camus wrote a novel about a European, *un pied noir,* killing an Arab on a beach outside Algiers. He works it so that the sun gets into the European's eyes (they have their rituals) and the heat and his emotionlessness to his mother's dying and all this. But killing an Arab, pumping successive bullets into an Arab, is not and never has been an alienating experience for a European. It was not unusual. It need not symbolize any alienation from one's being or anything like that. It was customary in Algeria, so how come all this high shit about Camus. Didn't it ever strike you that Meursault was a European and the Arab on the beach was an Arab? And the

Arab was an Arab, but this European was Mersault.

You want to hear a story? Let me tell you a real story. I have no art for phraseology, I'll warn you.

Ahmed. Ahmed. Ahmed. Ahmed came to the beach with Ousmane to get away. The town, stiffly hot, drove him from the bicycle factory, making an excuse to his boss. Headache, my little brother has a headache three days now. He needs the salt air. The grimy hands of the boss closed around a dry cigar in the tin can ashtray. "Ahmed, if you leave I don't pay for the week. That's it. That's it you hear." Ahmed retreating, feeling free already, sweat trickling and drying under his chin. He would go to the beach, Ousmane was waiting for him, the sand would be damp. Ousmane was at the corner, he held his flute anxiously looking up and down the narrow street. His face lit up as he saw Ahmed. "You got away, good Ahmed," running beside Ahmed's bicycle. Ousmane climbed onto the handle bars. Ahmed pedalled in the hot silence toward the beach. Nearing the sea, their legs and arms eased from the tension of the town. Ousmane's bare feet leapt from the makeshift seat at the same time that Ahmed braked. They headed for their favourite rock wheeling and lifting the bicycle through the sand, hot and stinging. Already he felt tranquil as the thin wind shaking the flowers. He dropped the bicycle, raced Ousmane to the water, crushing softly underfoot the vine and silky mangrove. Ahmed and Ousmane fell into the sea fully clothed, he washing away the sticky oil of the bicycle shop, Ousmane drowning his headache. Then they lay beside the rock, talking and falling asleep.

Ousmane awakening, felt hungry; his dungarees, still damp, felt steamy on his legs. Shading his eyes from the sun which had narrowed the shadow of the rock, his headache came back. He stood up, lifted his flute, and

112

played a tune he'd made over and over again as if to tame the ache in his head. After a while he wandered down the beach, looking for a foodseller.

Ahmed, Ahmed. Ahmed awoke, feeling Ousmane's absence at the same moment that he heard an explosion close to his ear. Ahmed felt his eyes taking an eternity to open into the glassy haze of the afternoon. A blurred white form wobbling in the heat's haze. Sound exploded on the other side of Ahmed. He barely raised his body, shielding his eyes as he made out the white form of a European. Far out in the ocean a steamer was passing. The sand around Ahmed pulsated with the heat and the loud ringing in his ears. Ousmane! Run!

Ahmed's vision pinpointed the white's face, the toothpick between the white's teeth and lip moving. The gun transfixed his arms. Beneath a veil of brine and tears, his eyes were blinded; they watched the steamer's latitude longingly. "Born slackers!" Ahmed's chest sprang back, tendrilled. "Born liars!" A pump of blood exploded in his left side. "Born criminals!" Sheets of flame poured down his ribs. "Born . . . !" Ahmed!

That is what happened! And as for Camus. Murderer.

This is it baby. The old woman has given the go-ahead. Now that they're all gathered — Rosa, the big white boy, the professor, the moneychangers and the skin dealers, the whip handlers, the coffle makers and the boatswains, the old-timers and the young soldiers. I'm going to kill them. I'll tell them I have something to sell. That'll get them going; it always has. Then we'll strangle them. It'll be a night for the old woman to remember. That'll make up for it. Then that'll be the end of it.

We chained them around the statue of Cristobal Colon, the prick-head. The old woman and I slashed his face to ribbons, then we chewed on the stones and spit them into the eyes of the gathering. When that was over and they were all jumping and screaming, the old woman drew out her most potent juju and sprayed them all with oceans of blood which, she said, she had carried for centuries. "En't is blood all you like?!" she whispered in their ears maliciously.

Then we sang *"Jingay. . ."* and made them call out everything that they had done over and over again, as they choked on the oceans of blood from the old hag's juju. Then we marinated them in hot peppers, like the old woman wanted. What an everlasting sweet night we had. The old woman was so happy, she laughed until her belly burst.

When Elaine returned from her continuous phone call, I convinced her to stuff the bodies in her trunk to Zaire. It wasn't easy, as she almost could not see me and kept saying how much my face had changed. I promised her the Queendom and riches of Songhai. She bought it. The old lady has promised me her big, big juju, so this is where the African princess and I must part. I'm off to see my new love and companion, the old hag of a banyan tree.

Note: "Ahmed's death" is intended to echo and counterpoint the corresponding scene in *L'Etranger* and therefore echoes the language of the Penguin edition, English language translation.

I used to like the Dallas Cowboys

I used to like the Dallas Cowboys. Steel gray
helmets, good luck gray, bad luck blue, skin tight, muscle-
definitioned thighs. I'd prepare for Sunday's game, beer
and my pillows at the ready. Rushing to the kitchen
between commercials, burning the chicken or the boiled
potatoes, depending on whether there was money, or
making split pea soup, scraping up the last grain of garlic
and the onions growing stems in the dark corners of the
cupboard below the sink. I'd neglect the dishes from the
night before or the week before, depending on the week,
set up a phone line with Tony or Jo as the case may be,
put the bottles of beer in the freezer, if I had beer, and wait
for the game, sit through the pre-game or the highlights,
have a fifteen-minute nap, time permitting. This was
after I'd just risen from an eight-hour sleep, most of which
was devoted to regenerating the body after dancing
and drinking till four in the morning. Whatever liquor
wasn't danced out had to be slept out. Naturally, sometimes even sleep would not produce the miracle of
waking up without a vicious headache and feeling water-

logged, but I had prepared for this by putting the television near to my arm.

Seems a while now, but back then, I used to really love
the Dallas Cowboys. It's funny what things occur to you
lying in a corridor at 3:00 a.m. in the morning in the middle of a war. Which is where I am now. The sky is lit bright
from flares and there's a groaning F16 circling the sky like a
corbeau. The flares give off the light of a red smoky dawn,
except for their stàrkness which makes you feel naked.
The air, seeping through the wood latticework, smells
chemical. A few minutes ago, before the flares went up,
the cat, who lives in the house whose corridor I'm hud-
dled in, ran screaming and scratching over my back. She
had heard the incoming planes long before they hit the
island again, on this second day . . . night of the war.
Having no sixth sense like hers, the rest of us dove for the
corridor only when the flares went up and we'd heard the
crack of the F16's through the sound of speed. I wasn't
asleep. Just waiting. Amazing how your mind can just
latch on to something, just to save you from thinking
about how frightened you are. It reaches for the farthest
thing away. . . . That's how come I remember that I used
to love the Dallas Cowboys.

The Cowboys shone, the Dallas sun glancing off their
helmets. They weren't like other football teams. They
were sleek where the others were rough; they were swift
where the others were plodding; they were scientific
where the others were ploughboys; they were precise
where the others were clumsy mudwaders; they were
slim, slender where the others were hulking, brutish.
Even their linebackers had finesse. Not for them the
crunch and bashing of the Steelers, the mud and squat
of the Raiders; they were quick, clean, decisive. Punters
trembled before the upraised arm of Harvey Martin, line-

backers dreaded his embrace. Too Tall Jones had too much oil, too much quickness for a defensive lineman, too long a right arm. It was ecstasy when Hollywood Henderson intercepted a pass or caught a running back for a loss. But most of all it was Drew Pearson, Tony Dorsett, and Butch Johnson who gave you a look at perfection of the human, male, form.

Mind you there were a few from other teams, like Lynn Swann, who was with Pittsburg. He was as graceful as the rest of his teammates were piggish. Sometimes, I think he flew. He was so lithe, I think everyone on the field stopped to watch him, this bird of beauty among them, so tied to their squat bodies and the heavy ground. He should have been with the Cowboys, really.

The Cowboys were fine. They had a move which befuddled their opponents while it raised something in me that. . . . It was when they were waiting for the quarterback's call. Hunched over, they would rise in unison for the quickest of moments and then settle in for the count again. The look of all those sinewy backs rising and falling was like a dance. A threatening dance. It reminded me of "the breakdown" which we used to do every Thursday, Friday, and Saturday night at the Coq D'Or.

Rufus Thomas started it with his song, "Do the Breakdown," and we just got better and better, perfecting the bend from the waist and the shudders to the left and right. Some of us added variations in the middle or with the hips and the motions of the crooked arm as the weeks went by, till the next new dance; but everything about Black dance was there in the breakdown. So when the Dallas Cowboys did the breakdown, it really sent me. I was their fan, the moment I saw it.

Seems like I made a circle with my life. Then, I was in Toronto. Now, I'm back here on the island, not the one I came from in the beginning, but close by. Speaking of circles, there is . . . was a revolution here and I came to join. Correction, revolutions are actually not circles but upheavals, transformations, new beginnings for life. I'm graying by the minute in this corridor. I feel feverish. That is a circle, ending where you began. The war outside is ending the revolution. We have nothing to listen to since the radio went off at 9:00 a.m. on the first day of the war, only the crack of the F16's over the house.

Rufus Thomas . . . tata ta tata tata pada ta pada pada boom . . . do the breakdown. . . . That was in nineteen seventy or seventy-one. Seems a long time ago now, considering. That's when I first went to Toronto. I was sixteen. I went to school. I partied. I learned to like football. Not Canadian football, American football. Actually it was Sundays. Sundays. I had never liked Sundays. Back home everything stopped on a Sunday. The shop was closed; people didn't walk on the street, except in quiet penitence and their Sunday best; and worse, the radio no longer blared calypso and soul music but Oral Roberts' "The Hour of Decision."

Canadian football was too slow, the downs were too few, and the ball seemed to be perpetually changing hands from one incompetent lot to the other, blundering up and down the field. American football, on the other hand, now. . . . Well, come to think of it, it was all the build-up, the pre-game assessment of the players, who was injured and who wasn't. You would swear that this was the most important event to take place in history — the tension, the coach's job on the line, and the raw roar of winning. When my team lost, I cannot explain the deep loss, the complete letdown which would last until Monday morning. My sister and I would remark to each other every so often, in the middle of doing the washing or in the middle of a walk,

"Cheups! Dallas could disappoint people, eh?" This would be followed by a pregnant silence and another "Cheups." The next Sunday, up until game time we'd be saying, "I can't watch that game, I just can't." But the call of the steel gray and the American star on the helmet was too much and Dallas! Dallas was good! You have to admit.

To be honest, if I really look back, it was the clandestine *True Confession* magazines from America which I read at thirteen that led to my love for the Dallas Cowboys. There was always a guy named Bif or Ted or Lance who was on the college football team and every girl wanted to wear his sweater. Never mind we didn't have sweaters or need them in the tropics, this only made them romantic items. We didn't have cars either in whose steamy back seats a girl became "that kinda girl," or a wife.

So anyway, because it was so boring in Canada on Sundays and because it was winter, morning, noon and night, I learned to like football.

And basketball. Mind, I always liked netball which was what they made girls play at Rima High School in San Fernando. And tennis, dying, dy. . .ing for Arthur Ashe to whip Jimmy Connors which he finally did at Wimbledon, which all north american sportcasters call *wimpleton,* which really gets me, like every broadcaster in north america says *nukular* instead of *nuclear* and they're supposed to be so advanced. Me and my sister couldn't bear to watch it, the tennis game that is, because we had already said too often,

"This Arthur Ashe can disappoint people, boy!"

Nevertheless we gave in. We were walking along Dufferin, that was when we used to live on Dupont, we were walking along Dufferin at Wallace and we suddenly made a run for Dupont after several long "cheups" and pauses and after hearing an Italian boy say something about the match to another Italian boy. We couldn't let Arthur go through that match alone. It was a battle of the races. Some people would be looking and cheering for Jimmy Connors. As we ran home it became more and more important that we watch the match to give Arthur moral support. Somehow, if we sat and watched the match, it would help Arthur to win. And if we didn't and he lost, it would have been our fault. So we sat in pain, watching and urging Arthur on, on the television. It was tense but Arthur played like a dream, like a thinker. Connors was gallerying, throwing tantrums like a white boy; but Arthur was cool. Connors would use his powerful forehand trying to drive Arthur to the base line, Arthur would send him back a soft drop shot that he couldn't make. Connors would send hard, trying to get Arthur to return hard, but Arthur would just come in soft. Arthur beat his ass ba . . . ad. I swear to God if we didn't sit and watch that match we would not have forgiven ourselves. This was like the second Joe Louis and Max Schmelling fight. Nineteen thirty-six all over again.

And boxing, I liked that too, and track. Never liked hockey, except when the Soviets came to play. And golf, would you believe. That's to tell you how far I'd go to escape the dreariness of Sundays in the winter. I'd even watch an old, lazy, white man's sport.

Last Sunday, here, was a little sad . . . and tense. Only, on Sunday, the war hadn't started yet. There was a visit to Mt. Morris from which you can see, as from most places on this island, the sea. Talk, a little hopeful but bewildered, that surrounded by water like this, one could never be prepared for war even if one could see it coming over the long view of the horizon.

The war was inside the house now. The light from the flares ignores the lushness of this island turning it into an endless desert.

I used to love the Dallas Cowboys like you wouldn't believe. How I come to love the Dallas Cowboys — well I've explained, but I left something out. See, I wasn't your cheerleader type; I wasn't no Dallas Cowgirl. I knew the game, knew all their moves and Dallas had some moves that no other football club would do. They would do an end around, which most other teams would think belonged in a high school or college game. So it would shock them that here was Dallas, America's team, doing a high school move.

I learned about American high school and college lore watching American football. In my own high school, where football was soccer, we didn't play it because I went to a girls' school. We played whatever we did play rough mind you, but it wasn't soccer. Football was played by Pres' College and St. Benedict's. Boys' high schools. Benedict's always won but Pres' was the star boys. This was mainly because they were high-yellow boys. Red skin, fair skin, and from good families. Every high school girl was after them, god knows to do what with, because there was no place to do it that I could find. Benedict's was black boys, dark-skinned and tough, tall and lanky or short and thick like a wall. Convent girls and Rima girls vied for Pres' boys, Benedict's was a second choice. Benedict's boys were a little aloof though; they were the first ones to be turned on by the Black Power movement. They stopped wearing their uniform right, they were the first to grow afros and get suspended or expelled from school for it. They were the first to have a student strike and a protest march around the school. Then they became popular, or clandestine anyway. Pres' star boys looked pale against them and everybody now started to look for the darkest Pres' boy to walk with, because the boys in Pres' who weren't red skin began to join Black Power too. My friend

121

Sylvia was the first to go afro in my school, and it was as if she had committed a crime, or as if she was a "bad" girl or something.

That year, the Black Power year, I didn't get to go to see Pres' and Benedict's play in Guaracara Park. But I heard it turned into a Black Power demonstration. Well truthfully, I never got to go but once that I could remember, my family being so strict; and anyway, I was always at a loss to know what to do with a boy after, which was supposed to be the highlight of the evening and anyway, I never had a boyfriend really. The other thing was, I really couldn't get into jumping around in the stands as a girl, not looking at the game and yelling when everybody else yelled "Goal!" All of us who would leave without a boy would walk behind our next best friend who had one, looking at her boyfriend and snickering. The girls who had boyfriends on the teams that played were way above us.

But this was soccer, which we called football, so I didn't know American football.

I really didn't like soccer until television came in, in Trinidad, and not until years after that when we got a TV and we could watch Tottenham Hot Spurs at Trent and you could really see the game and the moves. And we watched the World Cup and found Brazil was who we could cheer for, because Brazil was Black; and then there was Eusebio of Portugal who was Black, too. Now that's when the game got good. Pele and Eusebio made us cheer for both teams at the same time if they were playing each other because Black people had to shine anyhow they come. Never mind the Spurs, we wanted England to lose because they didn't have any Black players. That was an insult.

"What happen? They don't like Black people or what? They don't give Black people any chance at all?"

If the game was between two white teams, we'd root for

the team with the darkest hair. So Italy and Mexico were our teams. If it was British teams, the most rough-and-tumble-looking would be our favourites. So when TV came in, then is when I got into soccer.

Soccer didn't have any cheerleaders, but American football did. I was embarrassed when I saw them. They looked ridiculous and vulnerable at the same time. I suppose they were supposed to look vulnerable; but it looked like weak shit to me. Since I was a kid I had a disdain for that kind of girl or woman. I never liked not knowing exactly about a thing and I had always felt uncomfortable wearing a mini skirt or can can, when they were in fashion.

So I learned about American football. This standing around like a fool while men talked about football was not for me. Sometimes after Saturday night, and usually during the playoffs, someone, maybe Joe, would have a brunch and part of the programme was that we'd watch the game. That usually meant that the men would watch the game and the women would rap with each other (nothing wrong with that mind you), walk around, hassle, or humour the men about watching the game, or observe the new "chick" belonging to whichever reigning cock on the walk. Well see, I never came with nobody except that one time that I was almost married. But that's another story, thank God. I'd get a place at the TV and not without feeling that I was ingratiating myself and that I wasn't quite welcome. Well, I'd make some comments about what call the referee made on such and such a play and nobody would take me on. Then I'd get a rise out of them if I said that their backs moved before the snap of the ball. Well, at first they humoured me. Mind you the worst of them left the room, objecting to watching football with a woman present. Then they realized that I know my game, you see. I'd bet them money too, just to prove how serious I was. I out-

machoed the machoest. I yelled and pointed and called
them suckers, and then I'd laugh and tease them. Well, most
of them were Trinidadian, so they rose to the bait. You
could always catch a Trinidadian man in an argument
defending the most unlikely prospect and the most ridiculous outcome.

Before you knew it, everytime I lost a game, to be sure
that phone would ring and one of the guys would be
taunting me saying, "You see how to play football? Dallas is
dead, bet you ten bucks." I'd take the bet because the
Dallas Cowboys were magicians. They could take sixty
seconds left in a game and turn it into two touchdowns
and a field goal. Robert Newhouse, before he got injured,
could plough through a Steelers defense like an ant
through a hibiscus hedge. See, I wasn't no cheerleader. I
knew my game. Roger liked the Steelers cause they had
Franco Harris; but to me Franco was kind of clumsy. I know
he ran so many yards and everything, but when he started
to get old I figure he should have left, because he started to
look bad to me. Other people wouldn't say that, but I
didn't like the look of him. He looked too much like a
white boy to me, which is why I hated quarterbacks. They
were always white, except for James Harris who was with
L.A. and then what's-his-name with the Bears. Roger
Staubach I had to tolerate and anyway, he was clean. I mean
he could throw a pass. He could go up the field in thirty
seconds. Of course, one of *us*, Drew or Butch, had to be
there to catch it. But Roger was clean. Never mind he was
born-again and probably a member of the Klan, after all
we're talking about Texas, where they still fly the Con-
federate flag and all.

Another thing about the Cowboys, all my football buddies used to say that they were the most fascist team. Well
I agreed, you know, because football, or most any American

sport, has that quality to it. I said that was exactly why I liked Dallas because in this gladiatorial game called football they were the most scientific, the most emotionless, and therefore exactly what this game was about. I called my buddies a bunch of wimps. "How you could like football and then get squeamish? You got to figure out what it is you like, see!" Anybody can watch a game and say, "Oh I hate that. It's so violent." But they still live with it and in it. That person's just an intellectual. When I finally got to see the Dallas Cowboys in person, no set of intellectuals could have explained it, and neither could anybody who didn't understand the game.

To cut a long story short, because I probably don't have time for a long story, even though I loved the Dallas Cowboys, I had to leave the country. So I had to wean myself off of football because where I was going there was no American football. There may be cricket but certainly no football. It wasn't easy. You get used to a way of life, even though you don't know it. And you take everything it has in it, even if you think you can sift out the good from the bad. You get cynical and hard-arsed about the bad, in truth. So you find a way to look at it. So cynical and hard-arsed that when you see good, it embarrasses you.

The jets breaking the sound barrier keep rushing over the house. I've never ever heard a noise like that. Oh, my God! It's a wonder I can remember anything. Remembering keeps the panic down. Remember your name, remember last week. . . . There's a feeling somewhere in my body that's so tender that I'm melting away, disintegrating with it. I'm actually going to die!

Someone in the corridor with me says, "It's the ones you don't hear. . . ." Yesterday, we thought we heard MIG's overhead. . .wishing. . .we know that no one will come to help us. No one can.

I was going to another kind of place, much quieter. A cricket match now and then, maybe. . . . One Sunday, in March this year, I went to one. It was a quiet Sunday, the way Sundays are quiet in the Caribbean, and I slept through half of the match. It was West Indies versus the Leeward Islands. Cricket is the only game that you can sleep through and it wouldn't matter. They say it started in the Caribbean as a slavemasters' game. Of course, they had all the time in the world. Matches can last up to five days. They break for tea and long lunches and they wear white, to show that it's not a dirty, common game. Even the spectators wear white.

You can tell that it was a slavemasters' game if you notice where most cricket pitches are placed. You just look and you'll find them all laid out, green and close-cropped grass, at some remote end of what use to be a plantation, or still might be for that matter. Remote enough so that the players would have some peace from the hurly-burly of slave life, but close enough in case of an emergency whipping or carnage. If you pass by a cricket pitch in the Caribbean, not the modern stadiums they built but the ones that have been there forever, there's a hush over them, a kind of green silence, an imperious quiet. You will notice that children never play on them. They play somewhere on the beach or in the bush. See, there's no place to hide on them, which is why slave owners liked them, I suppose. While they had their dalliances there, they could be sure to see a coming riot.

Which, oddly enough, is why I left, here first, then there. I could no more help leaving Toronto than I could help going there in the first place or coming here eventually. I came to join the revolution; to stop going in circles, to add my puny little woman self to an upheaval. You get tired of being a slave; you get tired of being sold here and there;

you assault the cricket pitch, even if it is broad daylight and the slave owner can see you coming; you scuttle pell-mell into death; you only have to be lucky once; get him behind the neck; and if it doesn't succeed. . .well, you're one of millions and millions. Though lying in a corridor in the end, or for those lying dead, it doesn't feel that way, you're trembling, you lose sight.

So no Cowboys, no apartment buildings, no TV to talk about, not so much time to kill on a Sunday. Today, if it turns into day, it's not Sunday. What day is it? The red smoke dawn of the flares has given way to a daybreak as merciless as last night. Each day lengthens into a year. Another afternoon, God fled a blinding shine sky; wasps, helicopter gun ships, stung the beach, seconds from the harbour. Four days ago the island was invaded by America. The Americans don't like cricket. But deep inside of those of us hiding from them in this little corridor, and those in the hills and cemetaries, we know they've come to play ball. Dead-eye ship, helicopter gun ships, bombers, M16's, troops. I've seen my share of TV war — hogan's heroes, the green berets, and bridge on the river quai. Well none of that ever prepares you.

Because when they're not playing, the Cowboys can be deadly.

I've had four days to think about this. War is murder. When you're actually the one about to get killed, not just your physical self but what you wanted badly, well then it's close. I find myself having to attend to small things that I didn't notice before. First of all my hands and my body feel like they don't belong to me. I think that they're only extra baggage because there's nowhere to put them or to hide them. The truth is I begin to hate my own physical body, because I believe it has betrayed me by merely existing. It's like not having a shelf to put it on or a cupboard to lock it in; it's useless to me and it strikes me how inefficient it is. Because the ideal form in which to pass a war is as a spirit, a jumbie. My body is history, fossil, passé.

And my thoughts. I begin to think, why didn't I think of this? or that? I think, why isn't it yesterday? or last year? or year after next? Even a depressing day, any other day, a day when my menses pained me, occurs to me like a hot desire. I try to evolve to a higher form. I want to think out of this place where I'm crouched with four other people; but my thoughts are totally useless and I know it, because I think that too.

And the noise of the war. That horrible, horrible noise like the earth cracked open by a huge metallic butchering instrument. That noise rankles, bursts in my ear, and after a while it drones in my ear and that droning says that I'm not dead yet. I don't know when I'll get hit; the whole house could be blown away and this corridor which I chose, if I really think about it, and all the safety which I imbued it with. I would stand in the middle of the street and wave to the bombers in the sky to come and finish me off.

If I don't die today, the one thing that will probably dog me for the rest of my life is that I'm not dead. Why am I not dead now. . .now. . .now. . . .

I began well. I tried to make it decent, to die clean and dignified; but I don't want to die and my greed to live is embarrassing. I feel like a glutton about how much my body wants to hang on and at the same time it does not want to be here, in this corridor, in this world where I'm about to die. And so, in the middle of the noise, through the gun fire, the bombs and the anti-aircraft guns, I'm falling asleep. Can you imagine! I'm falling asleep. Each time I hear the bombers approaching, I yawn and my body begins to fall asleep.

Like now. Someone else in the corridor is watching me

trying to sleep in the middle of disaster. If we survive, she will remember that I tried to sleep. I will remember that she watched me, tears in her eyes, leaving her. We hum and flinch to each crackkk, each bomb. . . . We're dancing the breakdown. But if I fall asleep, I know that I won't wake up, or I'll wake up mad.

For four days now, a war in the middle of October, on this small unlikely island. Four days. I crouch in a corridor; I drink bottles of rum and never get drunk. I stay awake, in case. I listen for the noise of the war because it is my signal, like the snap of the ball, that I'm not dead.

But the signal is not from my team. I'm playing the Dallas Cowboys.

The day I finally creep to the door, the day I look outside to see who is trying to kill me, to tell them that I surrender, I see the Dallas Cowboys coming down my hot tropical street, among the bougainvillea and the mimosa, crouching, pointing their M16 weapons, laden with grenade-launchers. The hibiscus and I dangle high and red in defeat; everything is silent and gone. Better dead. Their faces are painted and there's that smell, like fresh blood and human grease, on them. And I hate them.

Sketches in transit
...going home

He had fucked one hundred women, he'd counted them, he was secure, no man could question his balls. His reputation was unquestionable among men and women alike. A real bull of a man, a man with his share of adventures. The scars from these shone from his body in between the bright skin. He took every opportunity to be amusing and dangerous. Now he swung his hips imitating the stewardess' gait. Ten minutes earlier he had said, within her earshot and that of the other men, that she was fat in the ankles but at the same time passable. He offered to buy everyone's Canadian money if they wanted Trinidad dollars. He had ten thousand dollars worth, he said.

"It have plenty money in Alberta," he said.

He had a paunch that women loved, he said. They couldn't get enough of him. The stewardess, he said, really wanted him, she was asking for it, look how she was leaning over him asking him if he wanted a drink, he had exactly what she wanted. A man with a good wood — twelve inches standing up. They didn't call him 'Iron' for nothing.

"I hear Fitzroy in Vancouver now!"

"Oh yes," she said, leaning across the aisle to the woman who said she knew her from home. She didn't want this conversation. Fitzroy, the son of a bitch, was probably doing damn good. It would wreck her holiday to think about him. He'd left her after getting his 'landed'. Thank god she hadn't been stupid enough to get pregnant for him, though it was close. Two summers ago he had come to Toronto for Caribana, but that was the last time she saw him. He was still looking well. He hadn't changed a day since the old days. Jasmine got up and smiled at the woman across the aisle who was beginning to say something else about Fitzroy. She escaped to the bathroom. She was going for Carnival. In the plane, now up above the office buildings she had cleaned for the last twenty years, she was going home. Like the rest on the plane, she'd saved for the trek every five years. Home! To be rich for two weeks and then back to the endless dirty floors at night and the white security guard trying to feel her breasts as she left the building. But for now, track-suited, tennis-shoed, photo-gray sunglasses perched on her well-coiffed hair, she flew the three thousand miles to the hot town, Port-of-Spain, with talk in the streets about oil dollars.

"I can't stand the heat now you know, I just break out in a rash; that is why I can only spend a week or two in Trinidad."

This she said to herself, rehearsing her excuses for running out of time and money at the end of two weeks. She'd head back to Toronto, to starvation for the next six months and her back bending over a mop, burning against the naked flourescent lights as payday crawled toward her.

They loved these new idiosyncrasies of theirs. Living 'away', they adopted them like children, eager to forget their past. They commented on them at every social gathering, rivalling each other for outrageousness.

"I can't eat my bread white any more."

"I would miss the winter if I ever go back."

"Life is much better here, yes."

"Alberta better, it don't have a set of Black people. That is why I like it there."

It was a sign of prosperity to lose the taste for home-made bread and to feel like fainting in the heat.

"Everybody's prospering over here, things so cheap it's no wonder."

It was a sign of improved class to live in a neighbour-hood without Black people.

The plane was full. Most, going home. For Carnival. They had arrived at the airport with their entourages to see them off. Suitcases piled high, stuffed with bluejeans, pots, microwaves, bicycles, toys, whiskey, electric saws, toasters. All the things which were the reason for emigrating in the first place, piled up, ready to go back. They had stood in line hardly looking at each other; jostling to reach the baggage check. The line stretched for one hundred metres, swelled by well-wishers, cousins with parcels for home, letters for mothers, strangers who'd come to the airport speculating that someone going home would take a suitcase for them. Here in the baggage line they were half here and half there, half reserved and half jubilant.

They hesitated before smiling with each other. They had learned hesitancy here. They had learned caution. It wasn't proper to yell each other's names across a street here. It wasn't right to blare music out of windows for neighbors to hear. Heaven knows enough policemen had come knocking on their doors for that faux pas. Here, all that was courtesy became insult; all that was human turned to signs of backwardness. They had traded boldfacedness for high-rise apartments. Going home, they sized up each other's clothing and hairstyles. Did they look good enough to have lived here, did they look good enough to return and not have someone notice that life here wasn't all that rosy. Did they look good enough to inspire envy. They waited for the doors of the plane to close behind them. They sensed their ordinary cheerfulness rising to be released. They knew it would be embarrassing to let go in the airport. Behind the doors they would breathe out the relief of leaving Toronto, that uncomfortable name of a city, where their lives were tight and deceptive. What a joy it would be to talk and have people answer, to settle into gregariousness and frown on reserve.

Ayo, noticing them in the baggage line and now sitting among them, was going home too. Not like them, she was really going home. They were going back as tourists for Carnival. Ayo was going back for good, but not to Trinidad. She watched them half with derision and half wanting to be one of them, to get caught up in the Carnival spirit. She, like them, had been grown for export, like sugar cane and arrowroot, to go away, to have distaste for staying. She had been taught that there was nothing worthwhile about staying; you should "go away and make something of yourself," her family had said. It was everyone's dream to leave. Leaving was supposed to change class and station. "You could be something," they'd said. This something was based on the exceptions who had returned, M.D.s or LL.B.s in hand, and had been elevated to brown-skin status; not like the rest of them "nigger people." To be something meant that, no matter what else. The majority of those who had gone away worked hard all their lives, without letters behind their names, without changes in the texture and colour of their skins, and had

134

not returned, but had sent messages in letters and parcels and money, enriching the myth of easiness and prosperity in the metropole. On the other occasions, on which Ayo had returned, she had found the myth alive and kicking and had made enemies trying to dispel it. No one back home believed that things were not better out here and no one could be convinced of it. People home would look rather nastily and accuse her of liking good things for herself and not for others.

Shanti Narine, gold bracelets from the Orinico blazing on her arms, spat food into her napkin. It made her ill, thick and gluey. It was what white people ate and she wanted to get the taste for it, but it made her ill. It was the kind that they put on aeroplanes to confound immigrants and third world people. She was afraid to ask what it was. "Quiche," she heard someone in back say. It looked green to her, *bhaji,* spinach.

Ayo, sitting across the aisle, smiled toward her in sympathy, then looked away to allow her privacy. They never let up, did they! If you thought you had their lingo down, they gave you spinach quiche to remind you that you didn't know anything. Then they threw in something with whipped cream on it so you couldn't tell whether to eat it or shave your armpits with it. And so in the middle of the plane you would make a fool of yourself and they would be able to identify you and take away your passport when you arrived or give you a curt nod off the plane, when they kicked you out.

Shanti Narine toyed with her food, put whitener in her tea, gave up on the quiche. She was one-quarter of the way to Bermuda anyway and, as delicately as she could, she spat skin and pit of a grape into her hands, fat, bejewelled, yellow gold of the interior. She said that one day she was sitting in her father's shop in Georgetown and that she noticed the Queen's face on the Canadian dollar. It was a face like a behind she said. Her sister Vidya had sent it, and looking at it she remembered her sister. Her sister had got the chance to go. Not she, because she was older and promised to a man in Berbice. She had only seen the man once, before their marriage. He was a fat little man with a giggle, like a young boy. She was disappointed by his look. She was expecting someone at least thinner. He saw the pout on her lips and said to her rudely, "Well, you not no door prize either!" and then to his own father, "Pa, I tell you the girl wouldn't like me." He stomped into the yard trampling on the zinnias which were hers, and the next time she saw him was on her wedding day.

Her little sister refused the little man's cousin and got away with it just because she was the baby. Her sister got everything that she wanted by behaving childishly. It never worked with Shanti. If she came whining to her father he always told her, "Girl, behave like a woman, eh!" But that's how Vidya got to Canada. She left to study and hoping to marry a white man. Both of which she had done. She had said that Guyana people weren't good enough for her, and her father agreed. But he had agreed to nothing for Shanti and stuck her in Berbice with a little fat man who raised goats and told her that she was lucky to get him because look how ugly she was. She'd run away from him countless times, except that her father would drag her back after a beating, saying that his days for minding big snake was over.

It wasn't that the little fat man was rotten to her, as much as he was boring. He said nothing, he did nothing, he just remained there like a lump which was plain, yet revolting. He was a sick yellow-green, somehow blending into the walls and the dirt. It would have been easy to ignore him, except that he was drab and she dreaded the odd night when he would roll over next to her, placing his clammy hands on her breasts. She lived with his drabness for fifteen years, bearing his five drab little children, until it was too much.

Now the flight attendant had her passport and everybody on the plane, she figured, must be in her business. Vidya had had to put up a bond for her to stay three weeks. Now she was being deported for staying a year. She should have gone to New York. Hell with Toronto! Who wanted to stay in their pissing tail place!

Leather-jacketed Tony Beard was going home until September to come back and continue at Wiilfred-Laurier doing business. He didn't like math, though who could, he always asked. But business was good to do, things were opening up, if you can't do business you're nothing in the Caribbean, for sure. He hugged his mother in the baggage line telling her that when he returned there'd be no problems, for sure. He'd cool his head and be more mature. She was proud of this light-brown child she'd made, thanked the lord that he had the good sense to go into business and love his mother at nineteen. In her prayers she beseeched that he marry a white girl, or better still marry into one of the French Creole families in Port-of-Spain. She'd denied herself and taken years of shit at the hospital. If anyone at home knew half the hell she had seen in Toronto since she left Piarco airport waving a white-gloved finger.

Her boy read a Toronto tabloid all the way to Antigua, lingering over the sunshine girl across from an article on the inferiority of Blacks. He agreed with the article, he thought. It didn't mean Blacks like him. It meant those "nigger people" his mother always referred to, whom he should "never, never have nothing to do with . . . all they do is drag you down," because he was light-skinned and

137

educated and different. His eyes hovered on the sunshine girl again. His lips pouted and opened, sucking in air.

The Canadians on the plane were pleasant, Ayo had noticed, since the baggage line. They looked people in the face and smiled, much harder than the faked skin-teeth smile they usually wrung from their lips. It had been the hardest thing for her to get used to or to learn. That meaningless jerking of the mouth into a smile which did not spread to the eyes and was gone in a second. But now they were smiling broadly, trying to catch someone's attention. They had suddenly become interested in Black babies, patting and cooing at every last one on the plane. Their eyes became uncertain, a little frightened perhaps, yet condescending. Ayo noted their Robinson Crusoe eyes.

He was confiding stories about how many women he had fucked and how many more he could fuck to a friend whom he met on the plane. His breath wheezing between his teeth. He was anticipating the fêting and the drinking and the bacchanal. His cock was like a weapon, he said, like a hungry animal. As he stood in the aisle he patted it and stroked it, made sure that it was there by feeling for it every five minutes. He introduced it to women with a movement of his hand lifting it and smiling. It would get a good workout for Carnival. He would press up against them in the bands of revellers. He could rub up against at least seventy-five in one day during Carnival. This was how skillful Iron was.

The plane had been an hour in the air. It was midnight. This was the Tuesday overnight to Port-of-Spain. They'd get to Antigua at 4:00 a.m.; Barbados at 6:00; Port-of-Spain at 7:30. Ayo was exhausted just thinking about the long ride. She would pass the time watching, reading, ignoring the blasts of calypso coming from somebody's ghetto blaster.

She hoped that the stewardess would tell whoever it was, to shut it off. Calypso music and clinking glasses raised such a din in the aircraft that Ayo felt more claustrophobic than usual. The honeyed, high, singing-talk of Trinidadian women spread through the huge cabin, aeolian in the artificial wind and counterpointed by the calypso. The men, voices staccato, emphasizing some spurious point about a Carnival past. The truth was that all of them were too tired to last the four days of drinking, fucking, dancing, and not sleeping that Carnival required; too old, not from age, but from living in another way, to remember their last Carnival in other than exaggerated phrases. The truth was that their living away so long had dulled their taste and criticalness about a good Carnival; had made the words a little stale and bitter in their mouths, dated in their delivery.

Fitzroy my ass! She was getting tight and sweet, downing a rum from the three little bottles of Bacardi she'd asked the stewardess for. It wasn't so much Fitzroy as it was how plain the thing was from the beginning. After this long, she was still vexed with herself for not seeing what was right in front of her face. Fitzroy was a rip-off artist plain and simple. No love or screw or anything good like that. A rip-off artist. He used to call her "Jazz! Jazz baby!" She hoped nobody home asked her about Fitzroy. She was going home to have a good time, not to remember fucking-Fitzroy. Fitzroy was an asshole and that is what got her vexed. Imagine, she getting messed up by an asshole. It wasn't good to be kind to people. Jasmine downed the second bottle of Bacardi and pushed her seat back, tapping her foot to the cabin full of calypso.

Ayo was going home. Not home to Trinidad, home to Grenada. Trinidad was actually home, but right this minute she could not identify with the affected happiness on the plane. She thought it was affected. She was a humour-less woman, short and severe-looking. Too humourless to appreciate the fêting mood and the good cheer which enveloped the cabin, too humourless to join in. They were fooling themselves, what were they so happy about, she thought. Stretching her legs up the aisle, she had discovered a friend, Diana, also going home. Diana had exclaimed in that long melodic woman-talk way, asking her if she was crazy not to be going to Trinidad for Carnival, when it was so close to Grenada. She'd smiled in a superior way, saying that she didn't know what Trinida-dians had to be happy about. She couldn't keep it up, she said. Diana agreed weakly saying, "But, you know how it is girl." They didn't talk about why she was going to Gre-nada. Ayo skirted the issue, expecting the usual disap-proval about the revolution. She didn't want to fight about politics. In this Carnival atmosphere it would be ridiculous to explain history. And besides, they were too big island/small island conscious to appreciate what a little place like Grenada could do. She'd be damned if she'd explain herself to this backward set of people anyway. They didn't say anything when Gairy the dictator was there, but all of a sudden now they were up in arms. All they could think about was dancing and bacchanaling; all they could think about was what this and that cost. Well it had made her sick living in Toronto. All people ever thought about was how much more they could get and take. With people dying all over the world, it was just sick, sick, sick. And don't talk about the rip-offs! How could she explain to these people that they were a bunch of idiots. They were so grateful for living away, when it was their sweat! . . . as if they didn't work! . . . as if the whole damn world wasn't built on slavery! Well if they were too damn stupid to see that, let them go right ahead. What the hell did they have to be so happy about? She wasn't no Trinidadian with them. She had decided and they had decided. She was going to Grenada and they were going to Trinidad. That was it. She begged off, walking back to her seat next to Shanti, and sat down, pouring more gin into her glass, wishing that they would get to Barbados fast so that the Trinidadians would leave.

They were becoming more and more uninhibited, the music louder, the laughter more infectious and elongated. Canadian anonymity was giving way to Trinidadian familiarity. The "oh jesus" and the "oh Gord darlings" were leaking out, spreading over the plane, restored to their eclectic meanings — "hell, I haven't seen you in a long time," "it's good to see you," "I love you," "you must be joking," "forgive me," "don't do that," and at least one hundred others. Now, over Bermuda, faces slackened by alcohol and distance from Canada, they relaxed into easiness. The accents returned, minding to keep that hint of "away" to impress friends at home. The Canadians on the plane were forgotten. They were too nervous to complain about the noise anyway. Not the revellers. Going home, they became more and more belligerent. They felt that they owned the airspace, the skies going south. Coming north maybe, the Canadians could tell them what to do, but not going home. They blared the music even louder and danced in the aisles. Even as the lights dimmed for sleep the two hours before Antigua, a sizeable, hard-core group carried the party on.

The small airport at Antigua lit up as they trooped off the plane. The tri-star, Trinidadians called it. They sailed on it as if it were not an ordinary plane and they boasted about it as if no one else ever sat in one. The boasting had become boisterous by Canadian standards. The entire group going home, more confident and assured.

Unsuspecting Antiguans slept through the invasion of huge tape recorders, walkmans, jheri curls, crepe soles (now called running shoes), digital watches, male sacks, pot bellies, Carnival, kaiso, intent arguments about american commodity items, who had what and what was more expensive than what, how much money who had, how much scotch cost and who didn't drink rum anymore, grand charges about the coming parties at the public service association and, lastly, insults at how small the Antigua airport was compared to Piarco and Toronto.

4:00 a.m. The rush of excitement came and left Antiqua like a lone Carnival band in Princess Town.

The first gust of hot sea air had washed their faces of nostalgia. All the years of talking about going home, promising not to live in Canada forever, swearing that they couldn't possibly die there, hating the cold and cussing the winter days, vanished. All the years of reminiscing about the food and the smells and the hangouts and the streets and the warmth of people, all the "only five years more," "only until I get a diploma," "only until I save a little money," all the "I could never live in this place," faded. They were struck instead by ambiguity as they stepped off the plane at Piarco. Love which was not love because it could not centre itself on a shape, a piece of land. Love which only recollected gesture and not movement, event and not time. They glimpsed, half-understood, half-seen, themselves. Wrapped in the gauze of hot sea air, they were silent momentarily. Useless as cash crop. Then, waving like sugar cane stalks in a breeze, they remembered, Carnival.

At 5:00 a.m. Ayo had left them thankfully, in Barbados, kissing Diana good-bye.

In the airport, waiting the three-hour wait to St. Vincent, she'd met a Guyanese man, Phillip Arno, and they talked about Burnham and capitalism. The man said that he was now a capitalist but had been a socialist once and she would soon find out about these islands. He said that he had been to Tanzania and Somalia and it was the very Burnham government that had sent him and, in every case, it was greed that fucked up the place. He had worked and worked and then they had him watched and threatened him and they turned the Guyanese national service, that he'd helped to set up, into a brothel. The ujaama villages never worked in Tanzania.

"Mental manual division of labour," she threw back in her best new marxist voice.

"Mental manual what? Greed!" he returned.

He was going to St. Lucia, anyway. His import-export business took him island-hopping. His neck was stiff from boarding houses. She was very interesting. He wished that he was going the same way.

"What was your name again?" he asked.

Ayo wondered why Caribbean men talked so incessantly and, getting a little carried away, suspected that he was an agent pumping her for information. After all, he used to be in the Guyanese army and had helped to set up the national service. She took his card. Asked him who he knew in Guyana.

He said that he wished the revolution well.

She doubted it.

He had made so much money in Brazil, importing and exporting, he was getting fat, he said. He'd look her up when he came.

She hoped not.

Ayo continued her journey to Grenada. She was going to a new home. Home had already begun, even though she didn't like Barbados. In the three-hour wait for the sun and the plane to St. Vincent, then Grenada, a short drizzle broke out in purple breaths of rain over Bridgetown. The sun coming up between the rain convinced her that she was home.

She'd always thought that it was stupid to die. She knew that the moment it happened, it would be like a shrug of the shoulder. Now it was confirmed. Flying over the Caribbean sea, in the LIAT, at eight in the morning, she saw a tiny sailboat below and the ocean purple all around it. If you just jumped out, you could remain alive for quite a while. Enough time to shrug, to find out how awkward and stupid the idea was.

A Brazilian woman, tall, slender, and brown, walking with a cane, smoked Marlboros, and a German man next to her read *The Advocate*. There was wealth in the woman's movements, in the man's heavy stomach. And all of it could plop next to the boat in the purple ocean. Ayo noticed tiny cockroaches in the fifteen-seater, and fifteen passengers. He moved again, the German bush jacket who got on board with the Brazilian woman, he was making her dizzy. The plane was small and treacherous enough without him moving around. This was the face, though. Distinct, proprietary. Yes, this was the real face of things. The bursting stomach, cheeks and bush jacket and the rich-looking Brazilian woman. It took years in the Indies to do this, Ayo imagined, to fill out his body so that it looked as greedy as he was. His mouth came to resemble a gesture of discontent at these people. It was right there, so that he didn't have to summon up the feeling anymore, just use his face as it was. Turn it toward the offending one or simply walk down a street. Everyone would get the message. Sometimes the whole damn island would get it, when his face appeared in the commerce section of the local newspaper or on the front page, a caption reading, "The executive manager of Geest has said that the banana industry in St. Vincent is in crisis, unless farmers produce a better quality product." Spread out on the plane, he waited to get there, to show them his face.

Ayo's stomach heaved on the take-off from St. Vincent. Would they never get to Grenada, she wondered. She asked the stewardess for a cup of coffee instead of the orange juice, thinking that it would help. The Trinidadians had kept her awake until Barbados. The morning sky, the purple ocean, had bouyed her into thinking that she was not tired or airsick. Besides, the work ahead of her would never tolerate feebleness. She was going home to own some place, before she died. She was determined to end the ambiguity. What had she said for years. When the revolution comes, I'm going to be there.

The coffee made her stomach worse. She had to go to the toilet. She got up, asked the man beside her to move, and went toward the rear of the little plane. The door to the toilet would not close, and when she turned in the little space there was an exit door which made up one of the walls of the rusty little plane. She jerked back in dismay. One slip of the hand while trying not to sit on the seat of the commode and you'd be out of the aeroplane, somewhere between the sky and the Grenadines. Back in her seat again, through the window, there was one of the islands that she was going to. She wished that they would land. It was the end of the rainy season but everything was still a dark green, except the sea which was aqua in some places and navy blue in others.

Through the window she saw the island. She could see a few houses dotted between the bush. It looked like a quiet place. There. Now customs, an hour's drive, and a small room to sleep.

145

. . . seen

The day was threatening to be a real scorcher. If she didn't have to go to work, she'd lie there on the floor where it was cool or go to the beach. She knew that by one o'clock she'd be sleepy and harrassed and hot. She took a cold shower and put on the lightest garment that she could find. As she walked the ten minutes to the office, water from her wet hair fell to her forehead and shoulders. She said good morning to someone. There were so few people on the island that you had to say good morning to everyone or else they would be offended. It was impossible to look at the sun. This island was amazing, she remarked to herself, as she took the lane with houses only to one side.

The earth smell, acrid and thick, was always in the nostrils. Every living thing here went to extremes. There wasn't one good reason why flowers should be so red and leaves so green. The pressing sky and the fecund earth were sometimes unbearable. Insistent almost on a life where difficulty marked the body and finally the face. Every morning, facing the sky and the earth was a present challenge.

Looking at the faces passing her, she recognized the excuses for her continual thoughts of flight. The island threw her, them, into a battle against fear and hope. They hacked the land with machetes and footfalls, only to see it grow over come the rainy season and the sky changing faces, reflecting opposite impressions to the place below. In the rainy season the sky is not as flamboyant. But no less dangerous. Deluged, the rain's water washes all colour out of it. The blues are lighter, the pinks, less bloody. It is no longer at arm's length and, in the evenings, the sun sinks, docile from the day's rivalry with the clouds. Some days, her mouth would drop open at the sight of the sky. She could spend all day looking at it, hoping that it would unravel something of its purpose.

Here, the inevitable conflict was with the sky. It seemed closer, red as a hot-veined kiss. The face you'd turn to, to find an answer.

She had come home to work and work she had. Every day, awake at five, office by eight, working late, beach, then home by eight, sleep, if she could, by twelve. When the work took her up the islands, she'd sit in the eight-seater island hopper, so small against the sky. Her severity eased — was forced, coaxed to ease with the waiting in lines, the walking for miles, the rub and smell of market women, the trail and skip of children, the patient sun, the custom of everyone living by the day and the night and not by the artifice of wealth or superiority.

Sometimes at night, sitting at her small table with the lamp, the most exotic of insects passed in her presence. Beetles with anteater heads and antlers, mosquitoes with fat bellies of blood and sharp bites, the greenest, smallest and softest of grasshoppers, slow, small-winged, heavy-bottomed fruitflies, all the most absurd shaped and coloured creatures this island had to offer. Sometimes she spared their lives. At other times she killed them and thought that she would be punished in another life. So she tried to kill them without malice. But there was a closeness in their appearance, a humility in a place where pesticides could not be purchased cheaply and fecundity rose in the smell of all things rotten and decaying and ripening to be eaten. Such noises at night, such singing, neither gay nor sad. Frogs and crickets and indescribably green and crawling, flying beasts. Singing, for nothing, just to pass the night. Like her not singing, listening, coming home.

The night, whose morning found her on the floor, a bird woke her up. It screamed at around 1:00 a.m. Screamed and beat its wings across the top of the house. She jumped out of bed, thinking that it was a burglar and stayed awake all night. It was not long since she had fallen asleep. Another one of her long nights. Her nights were hardest, had always been, at home. Their blackness could be mistaken for smoke, so thick and billowing, and the mornings took long to come. What was she doing on the island, why had she come?

In the mornings she was still awake. The beasts outside stopped crying or singing, and she fell asleep until the sun heated up and the flies began their buzzing around her face and left ear. Day noises did not startle her or fill her with as much wonder and fear. The sun blazed through the intermittent rain. Then, in the evenings, it sank below the level of the eyes signalling the singing and crying. At night, she locked the doors and the windows upon the first sound of singing. Suddenly the area between the door and the yard became wild, without order or control. All the things which she knew in the day, their positions, their shapes, became unknown. In the mornings, she would find them in their day places. The sugar apple tree, the corn, the breadfruit tree with its massive fruit and leaves. There, where they had been the day before. She laughed at herself each morning. Each morning, science and logic asserted themselves. At night they faded into fear and superstition.

A candle, a box of matches lay on the table with the lamp. The bottle of rum half empty stood next to them. She had drunk half of it and still had not slept after the bird had frightened her awake. She and the dogs barking at their shadows had kept vigil all night long.

She had come home. A year ago now. To live here, to understand this.

Other titles from Firebrand Books include:

The Big Mama Stories by Shay Youngblood/$8.95

A Burst Of Light, Essays by Audre Lorde/$7.95

Diamonds Are A Dyke's Best Friend by Yvonne Zipter/$9.95

Dykes To Watch Out For, Cartoons by Alison Bechdel/$6.95

Eye Of A Hurricane, Stories by Ruthann Robson / $8.95

The Fires Of Bride, A Novel by Ellen Galford/$8.95

A Gathering Of Spirit, A Collection by North American Indian Women edited by Beth Brant *(Degonwadonti)*/$9.95

Getting Home Alive by Aurora Levins Morales and Rosario Morales/$8.95

Good Enough To Eat, A Novel by Lesléa Newman/$8.95

Humid Pitch, Narrative Poetry by Cheryl Clarke/$8.95

Jonestown & Other Madness, Poetry by Pat Parker/$5.95

The Land Of Look Behind, Prose and Poetry by Michelle Cliff/$6.95

A Letter To Harvey Milk, Short Stories by Lesléa Newman/$8.95

Letting In The Night, A Novel by Joan Lindau/$8.95

Living As A Lesbian, Poetry by Cheryl Clarke/$6.95

Making It, A Woman's Guide to Sex in the Age of AIDS by Cindy Patton and Janis Kelly/$3.95

Metamorphosis, Reflections On Recovery, by Judith McDaniel/$7.95

Mohawk Trail by Beth Brant *(Degonwadonti)*/$6.95

Moll Cutpurse, A Novel by Ellen Galford/$7.95

More Dykes To Watch Out For, Cartoons by Alison Bechdel/$7.95

The Monarchs Are Flying, A Novel by Marion Foster/$8.95

My Mama's Dead Squirrel, Lesbian Essays on Southern Culture by Mab Segrest/$8.95

The Other Sappho, A Novel by Ellen Frye/$8.95

Politics Of The Heart, A Lesbian Parenting Anthology edited by Sandra Pollack and Jeanne Vaughn/$11.95

Presenting. . . Sister NoBlues by Hattie Gossett/$8.95

A Restricted Country by Joan Nestle/$8.95

Sanctuary, A Journey by Judith McDaniel/$7.95

Shoulders, A Novel by Georgia Cotrell/$8.95

The Sun Is Not Merciful, Short Stories by Anna Lee Walters/$7.95

Tender Warriors, A Novel by Rachel Guido deVries/$7.95

This Is About Incest by Margaret Randall/$7.95

(continued)

The Threshing Floor, Short Stories by Barbara Burford/$7.95

Trash, Stories by Dorothy Allison/$8.95

The Women Who Hate Me, Poetry by Dorothy Allison/$5.95

Words To The Wise, A Writer's Guide to Feminist and Lesbian Periodicals & Publishers by Andrea Fleck Clardy/$3.95

Yours In Struggle, Three Feminist Perspectives on Anti-Semitism and Racism by Elly Bulkin, Minnie Bruce Pratt, and Barbara Smith/$8.95